THE SUPER FRIENDS SAVE CHRISTMAS!

By Billy Wrecks • Based on a story by J. E. Bright • Illustrated by Min S. Ku

Random House 🏠 New York

Copyright © 2012 DC Comics.
DC SUPER FRIENDS and all related characters and elements are trademarks of and © DC Comics.
(s12)

RHUS26681

Published in the United States by Random House Children's Books, a division of Random House, Inc., 1745 Broadway, New York, NY 10019, and in Canada by Random House of Canada Limited, Toronto. Random House and the colophon are registered trademarks of Random House, Inc.

ISBN: 978-0-307-97946-9   randomhouse.com/kids   dckids.kidswb.com   MANUFACTURED IN CHINA

10 9 8 7 6 5 4 3 2

It was almost Christmas. Batman, Green Lantern, Robin, and Superman were busy helping some of their young friends get ready for Santa's yearly visit.

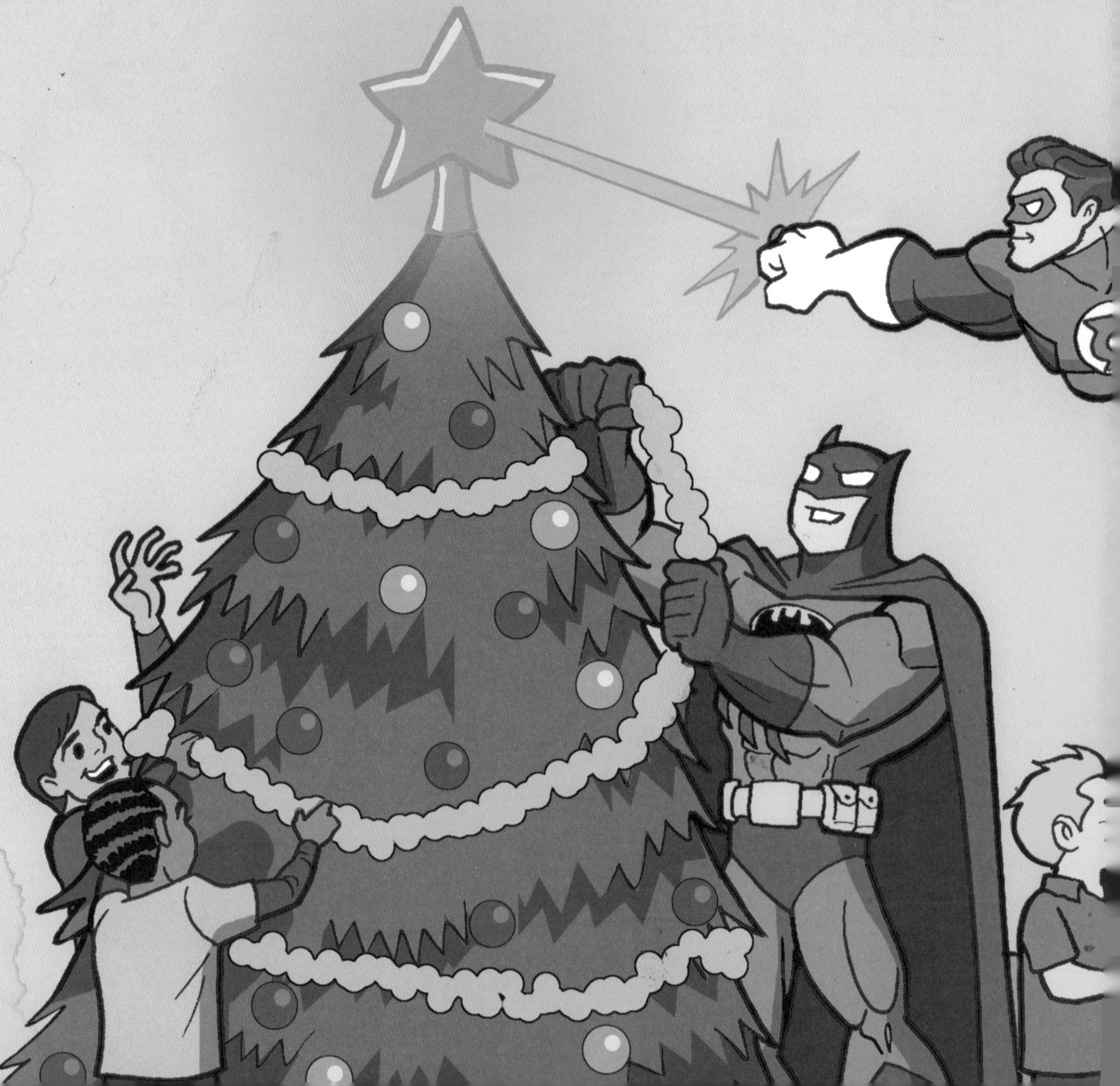

"Santa will be here soon, won't he?" one of the children asked.

"That's right," Green Lantern said. He used his power ring to create a glowing green star on top of the tree.

But Batman wasn't so sure. It was getting late and there still was no sign of Santa.

Batman whispered to Superman, "You and the Flash had better take a quick look for him."

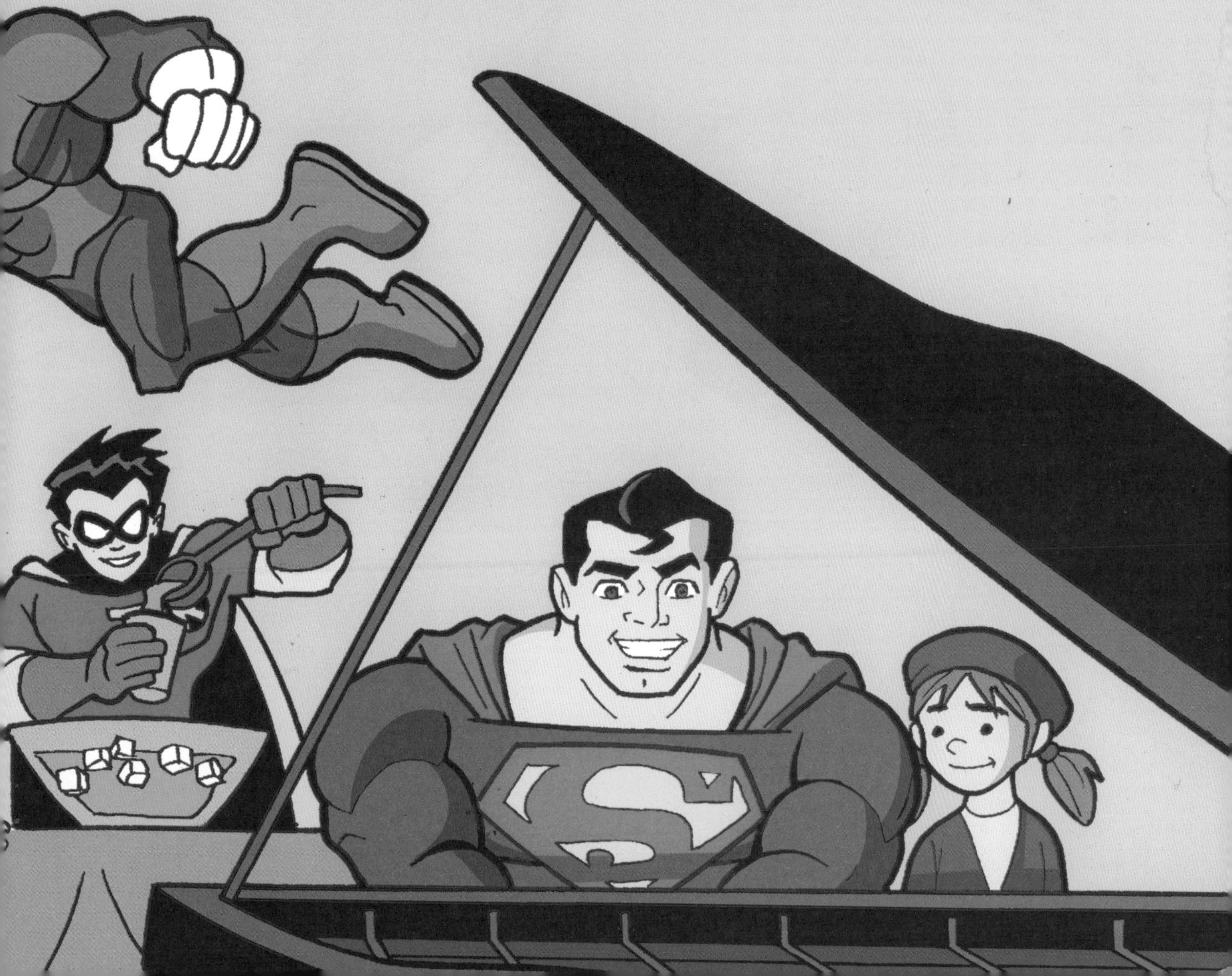

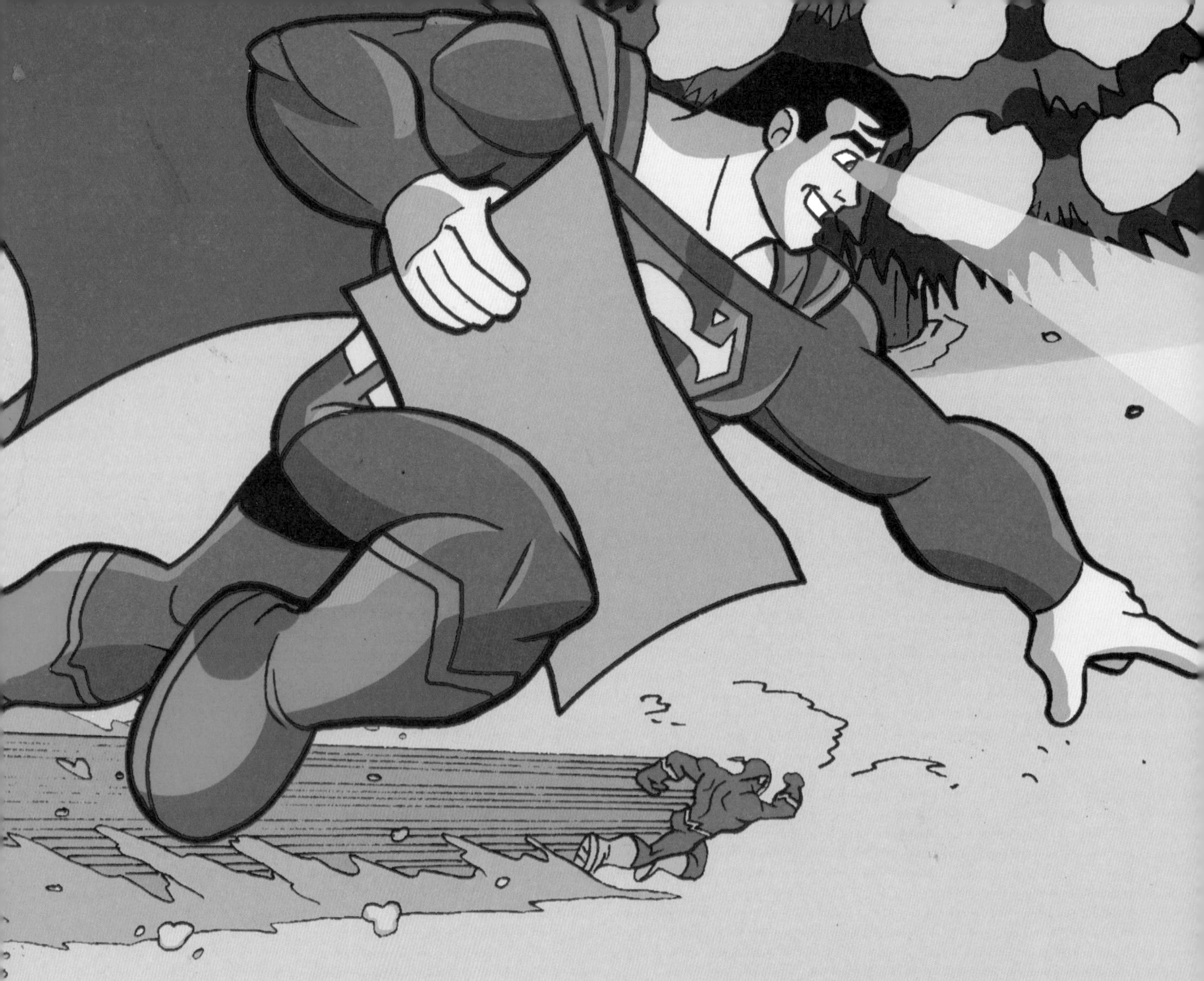

"I think we should head north," Superman said, following a map and using his super-hearing to locate the sound of sleigh bells.

"You did it, Superman!" the Flash cheered. "There's Santa's sleigh, on a roof."

"Uh-oh, I see trouble," Superman said, looking inside the house with his X-ray vision. "I think the Joker is being extra-naughty this Christmas."

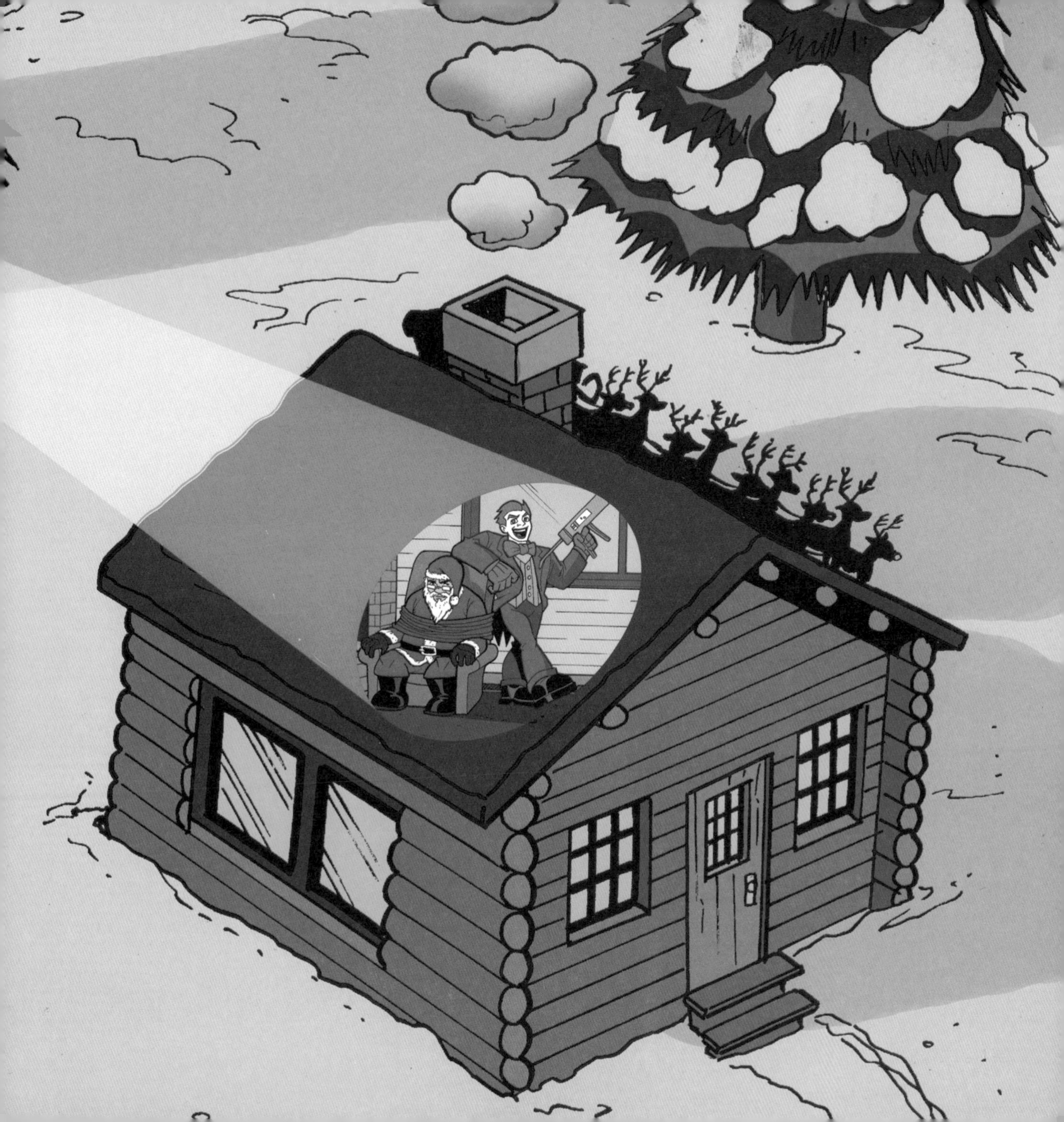

"Lex Luthor gave me some Kryptonite for being such a bad boy," the Joker said, spraying Superman with a sticky substance. "And I knew just what to do with it—make superglue for a super Goody Two-shoes!"

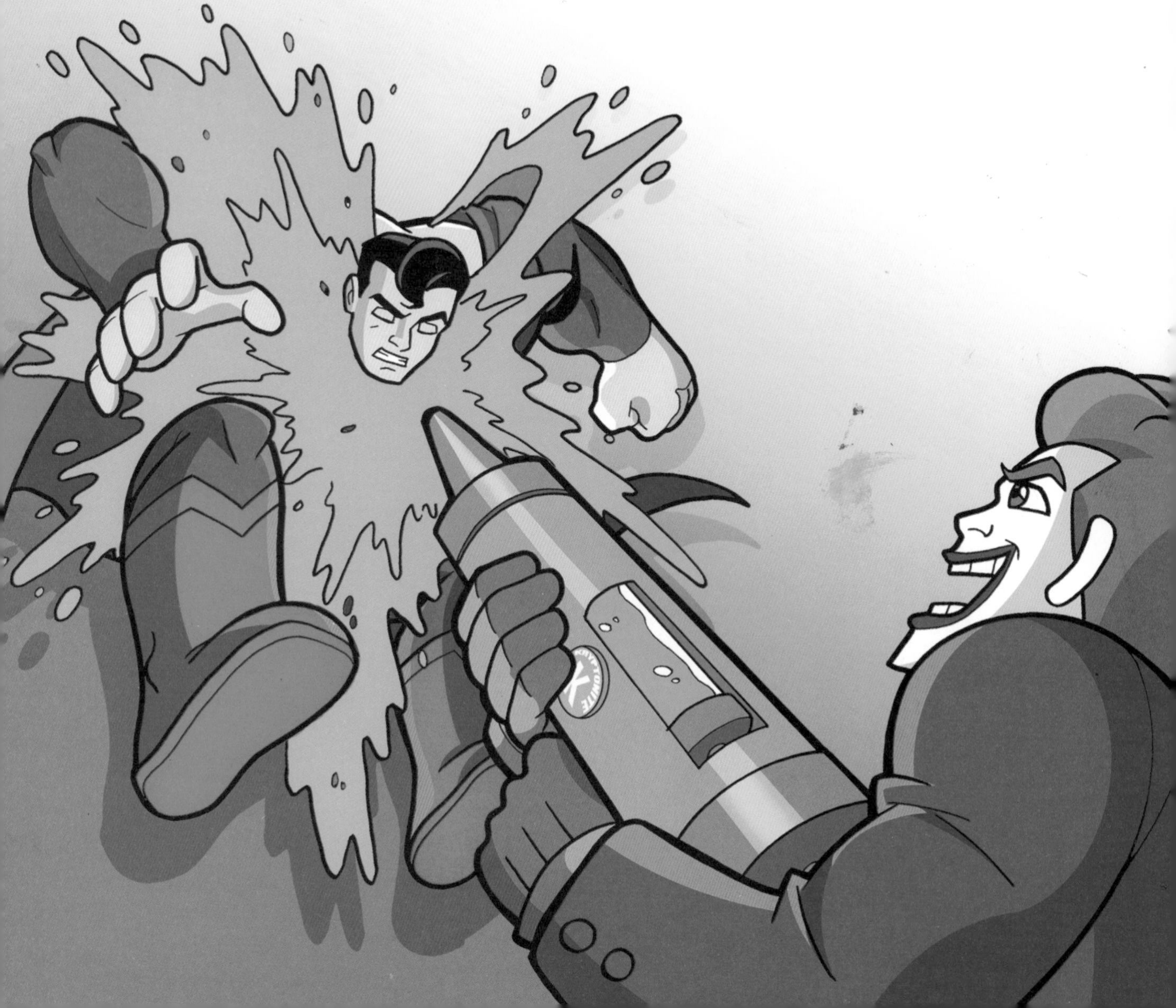
KRYPTONITE

"Oh, no! Kryptonite is the only thing that can stop Superman!" the Flash cried. "Don't worry, I'll save—"

But the Joker sprayed the Flash's feet with the sticky stuff, too. The Flash was stuck to the floor!

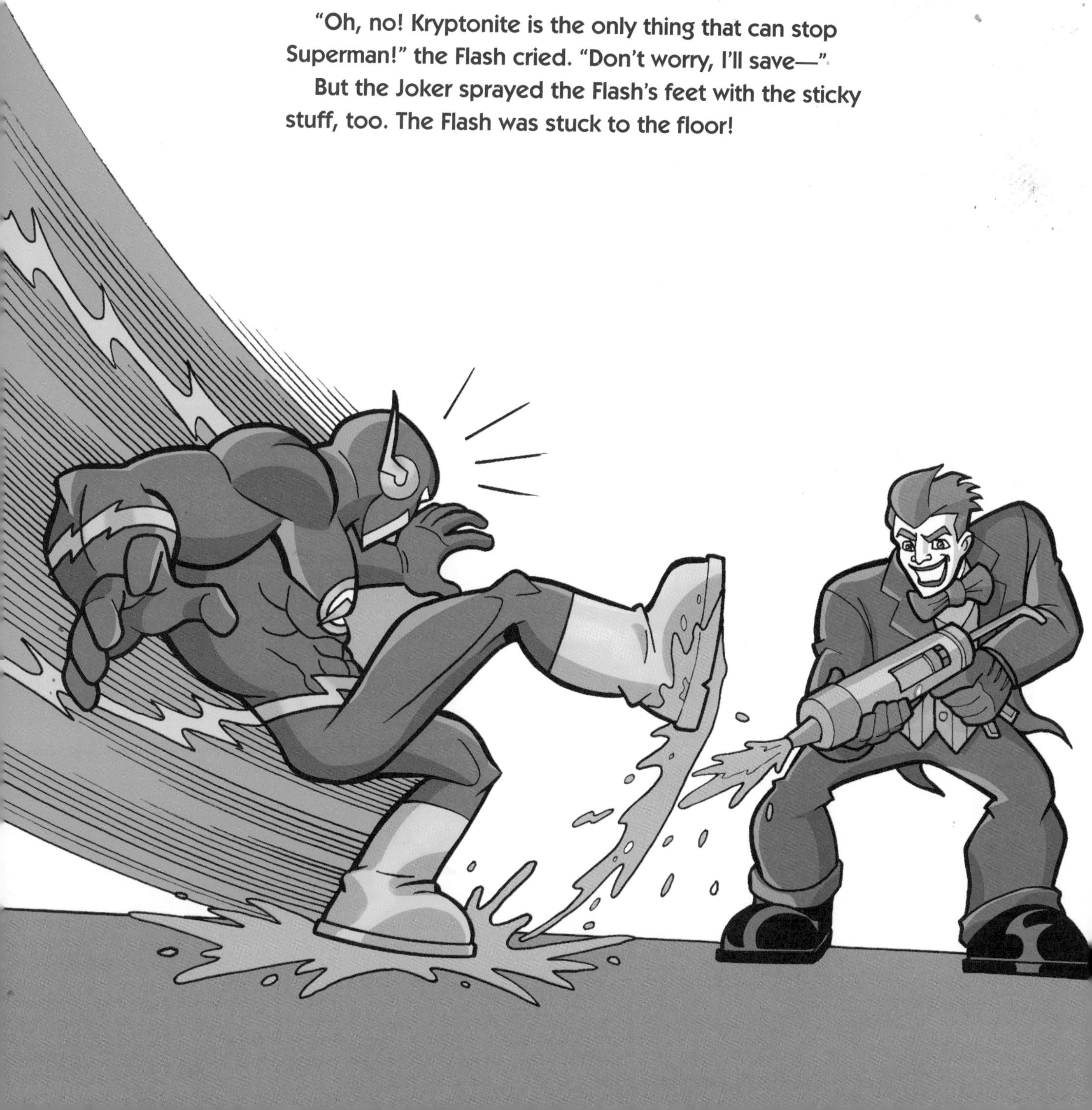

"Ha! Ha! Ha!" the Joker laughed. "I've stopped the Super Friends and Christmas. It's my best joke yet!"

"Ho! Ho! Ho!" Santa chuckled. "You can tie me up, but you can't really stop Christmas!"

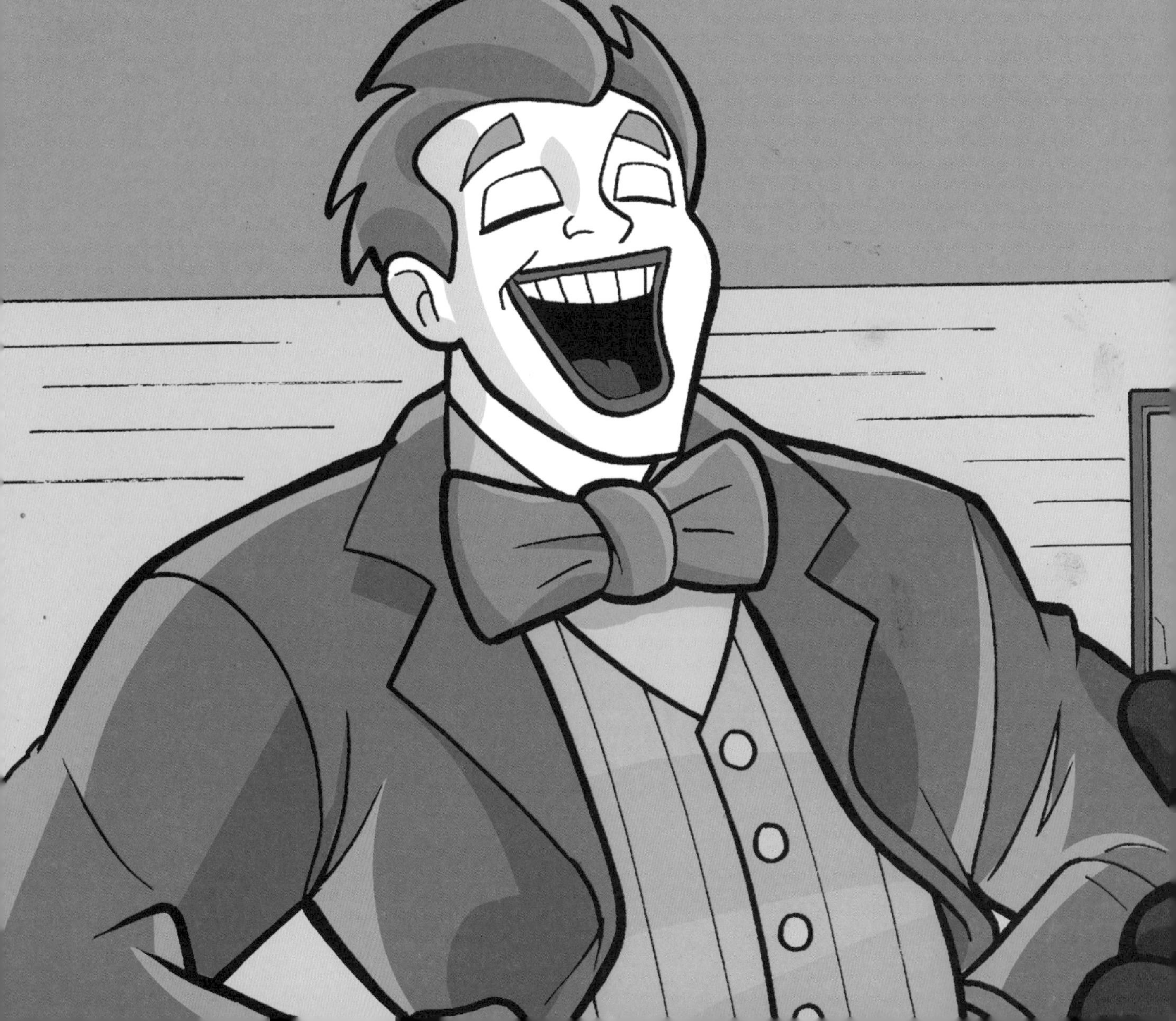

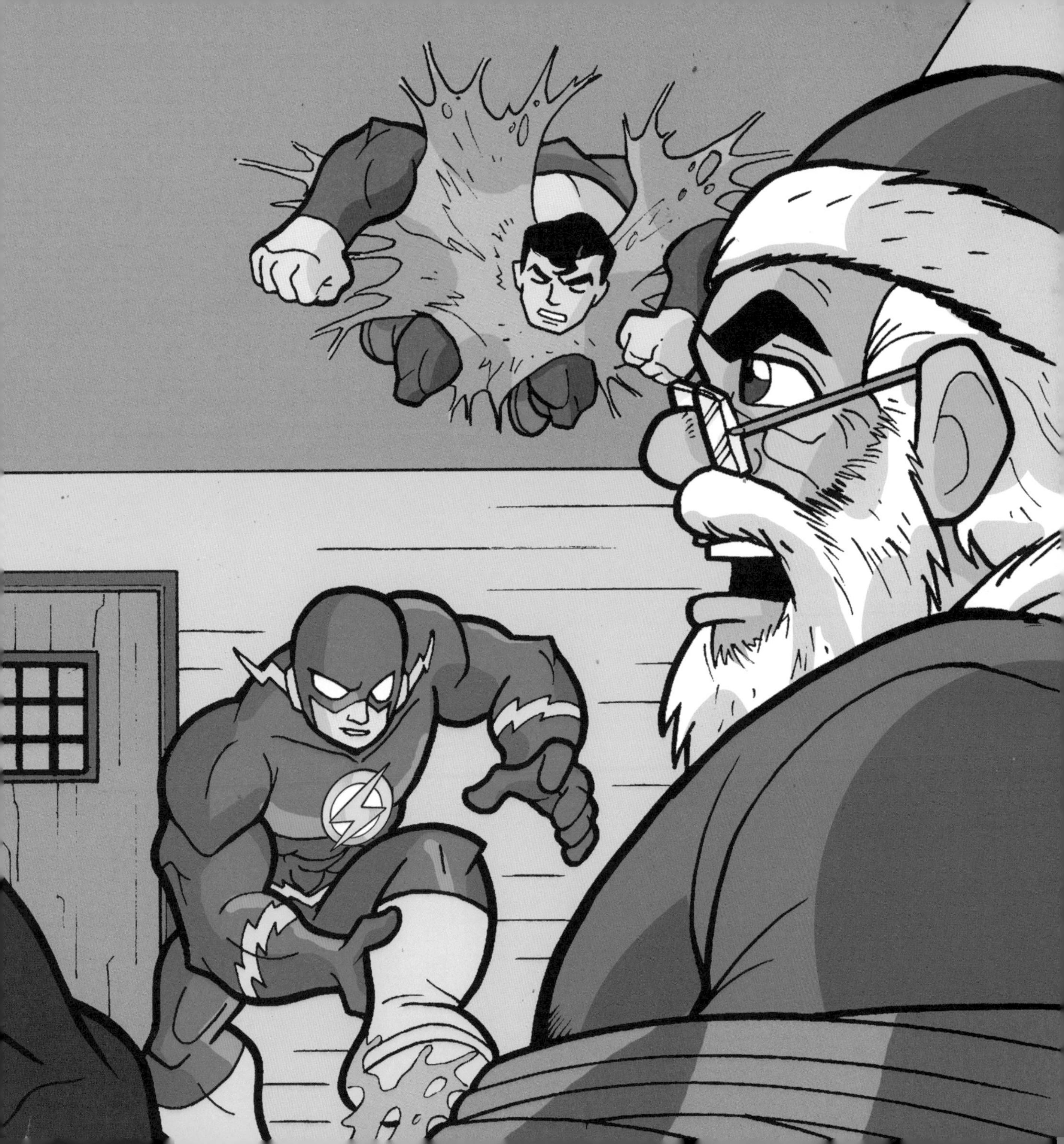

Santa was right! Batman and Green Lantern had followed their friends. Batman used the laser from his Utility Belt to free the Flash and Superman. "Thanks, friend!" the Flash exclaimed, pulling his feet out of the sticky mess.

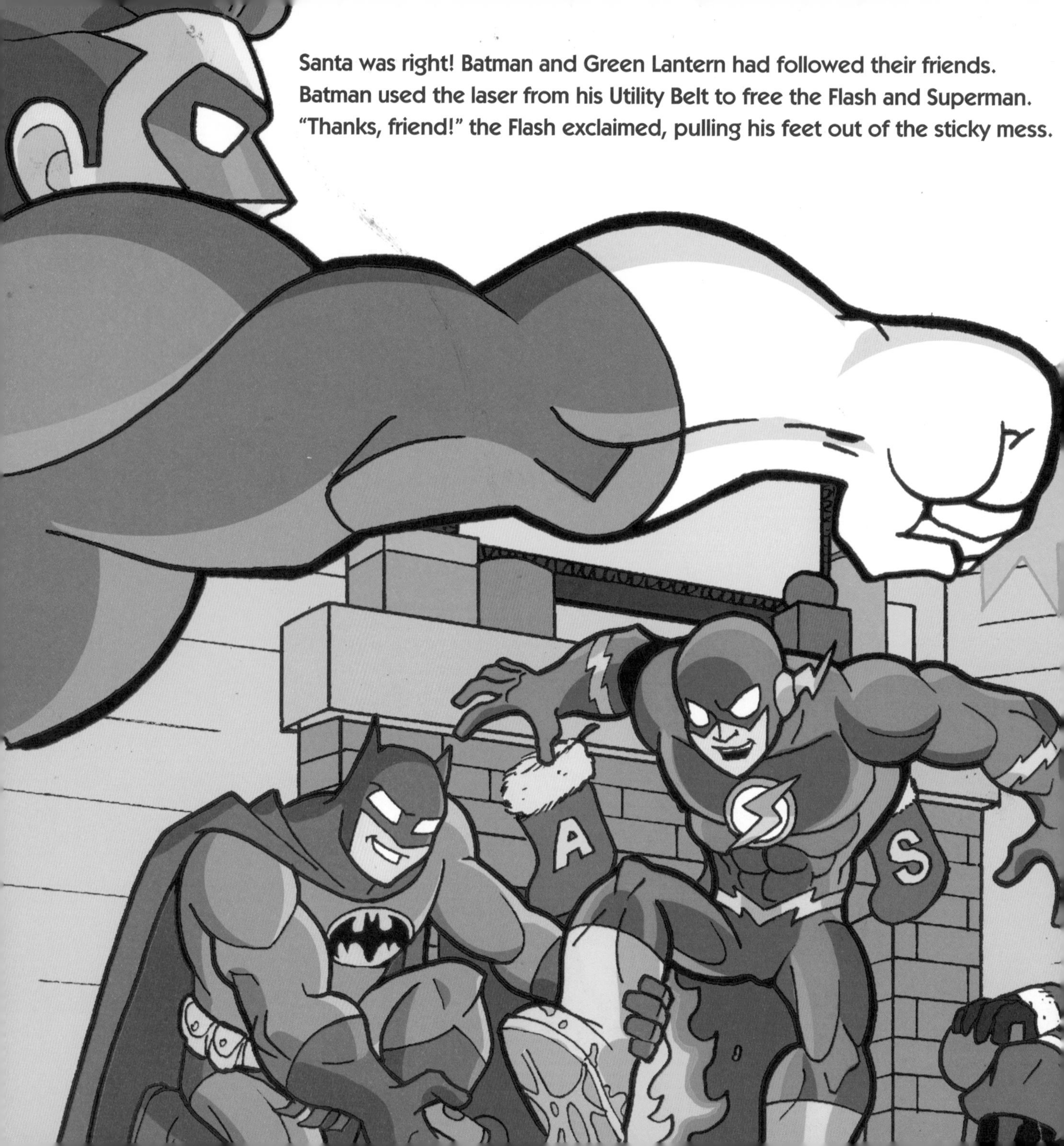
A
S

"The joke's on you, Joker!" Green Lantern said as he used his power ring to spray the Joker's glue back at him.

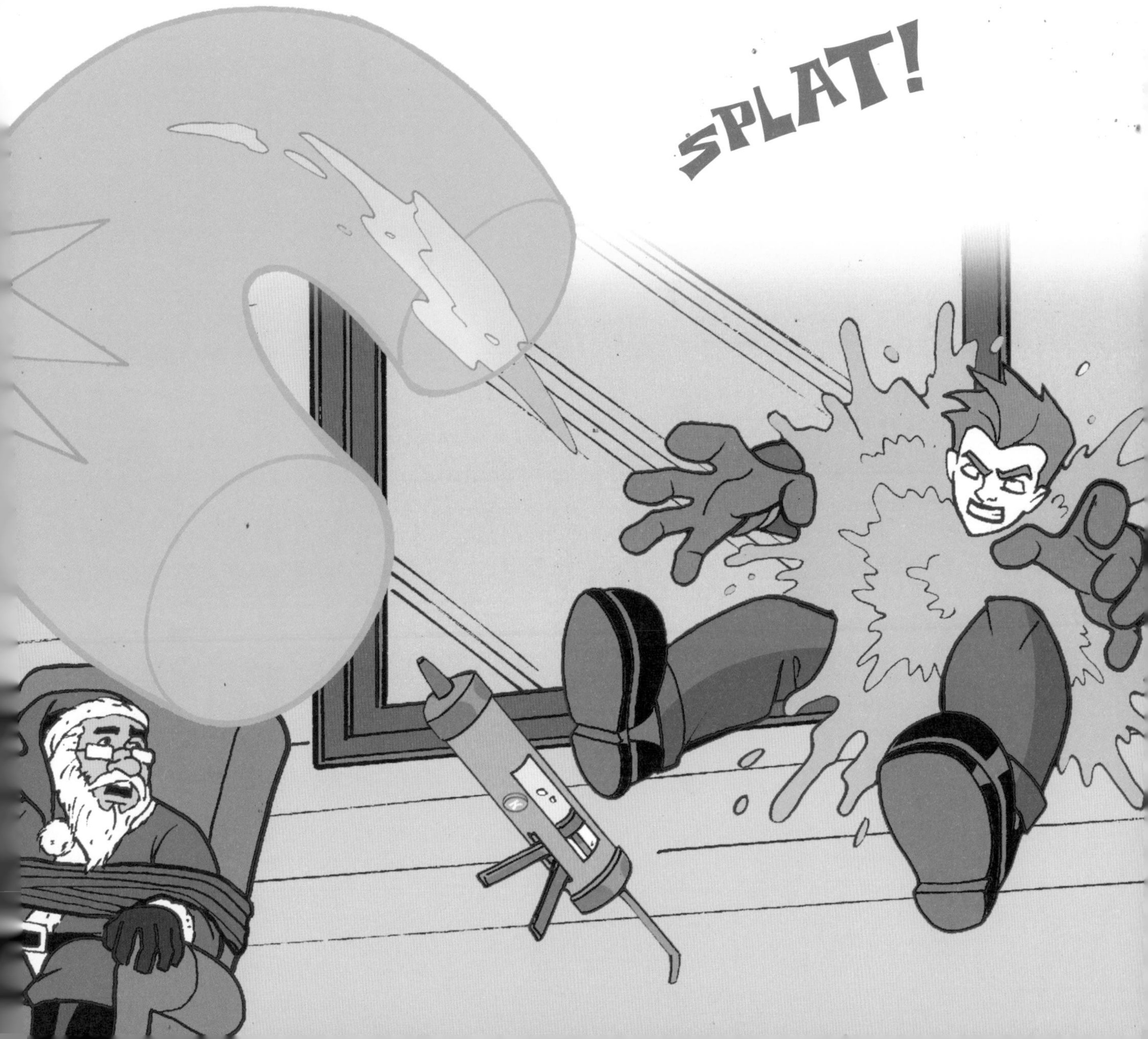
SPLAT!

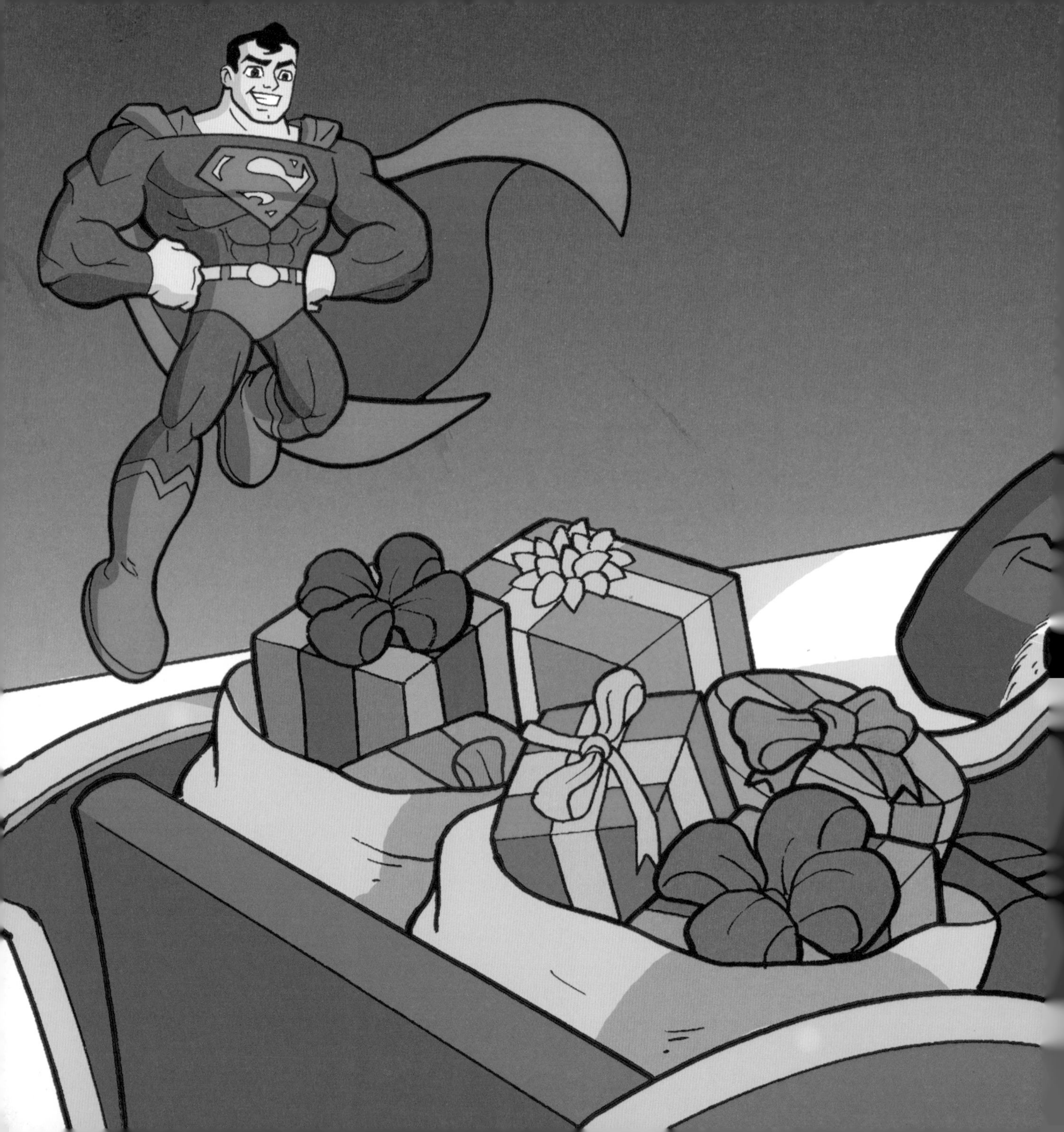

"Let's hurry! I've got presents to deliver!" Santa exclaimed. "Oh, no! The Joker ruined the reins on my sleigh. Now I can't fly!"

"Don't worry," Superman said with a jolly laugh. "Your reindeer can take the night off. I have an idea!"

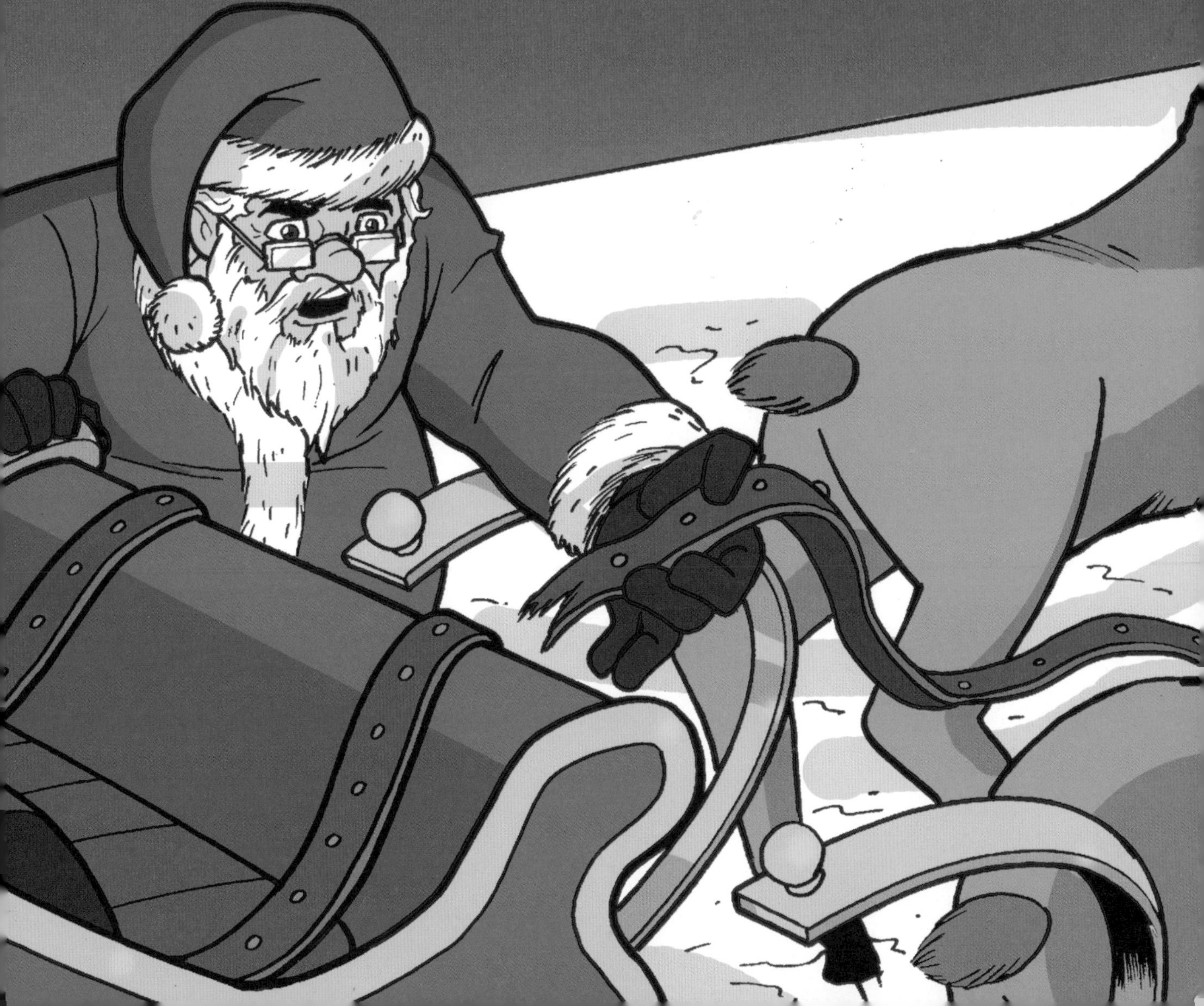

Superman used his super-strength to lift Santa's sleigh, and then he took off into the night!

"The Super Friends will help you deliver all the presents," Batman told Santa.

"Woo-hoo!" the Flash cheered. "I feel just like Santa in my red suit!"

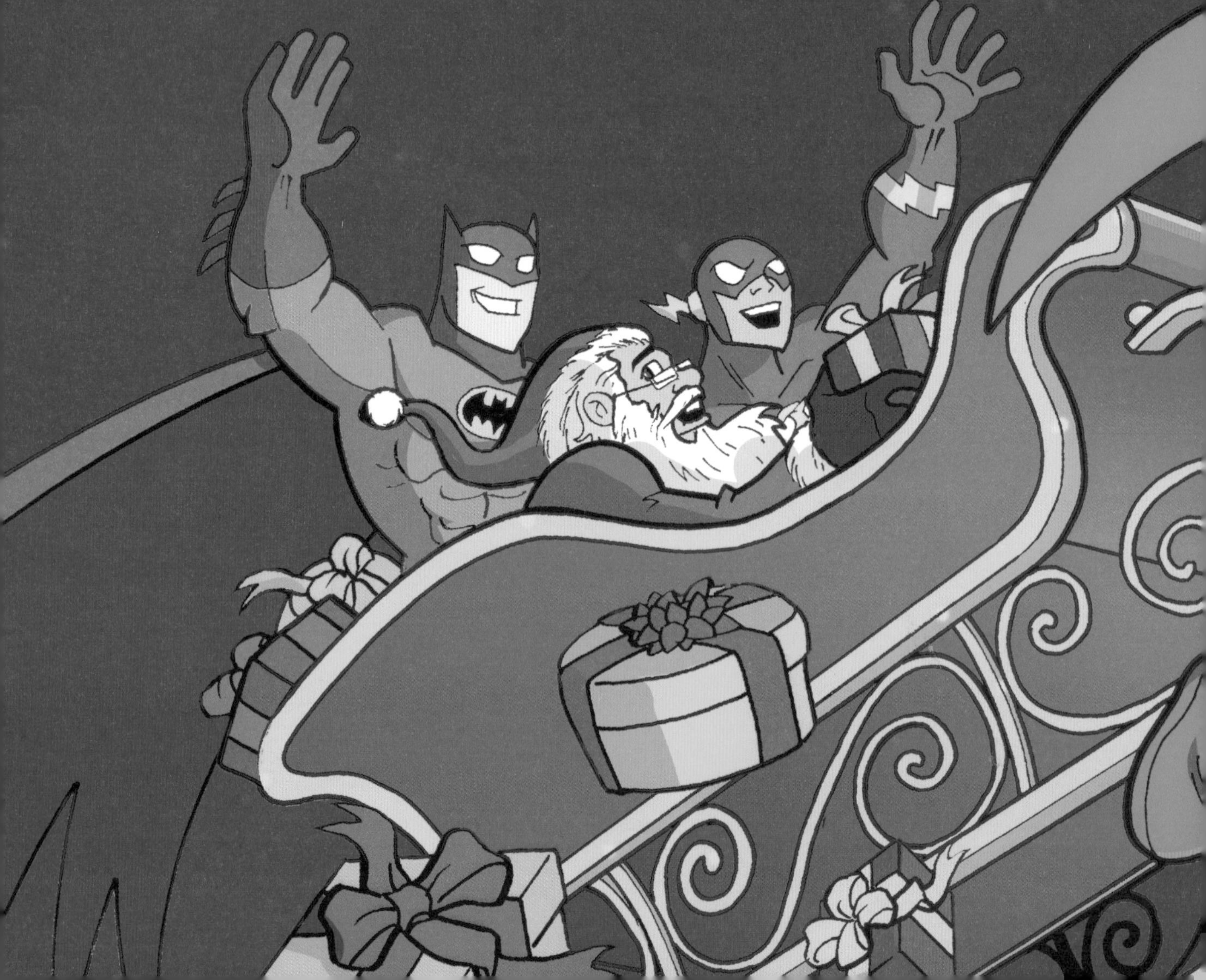

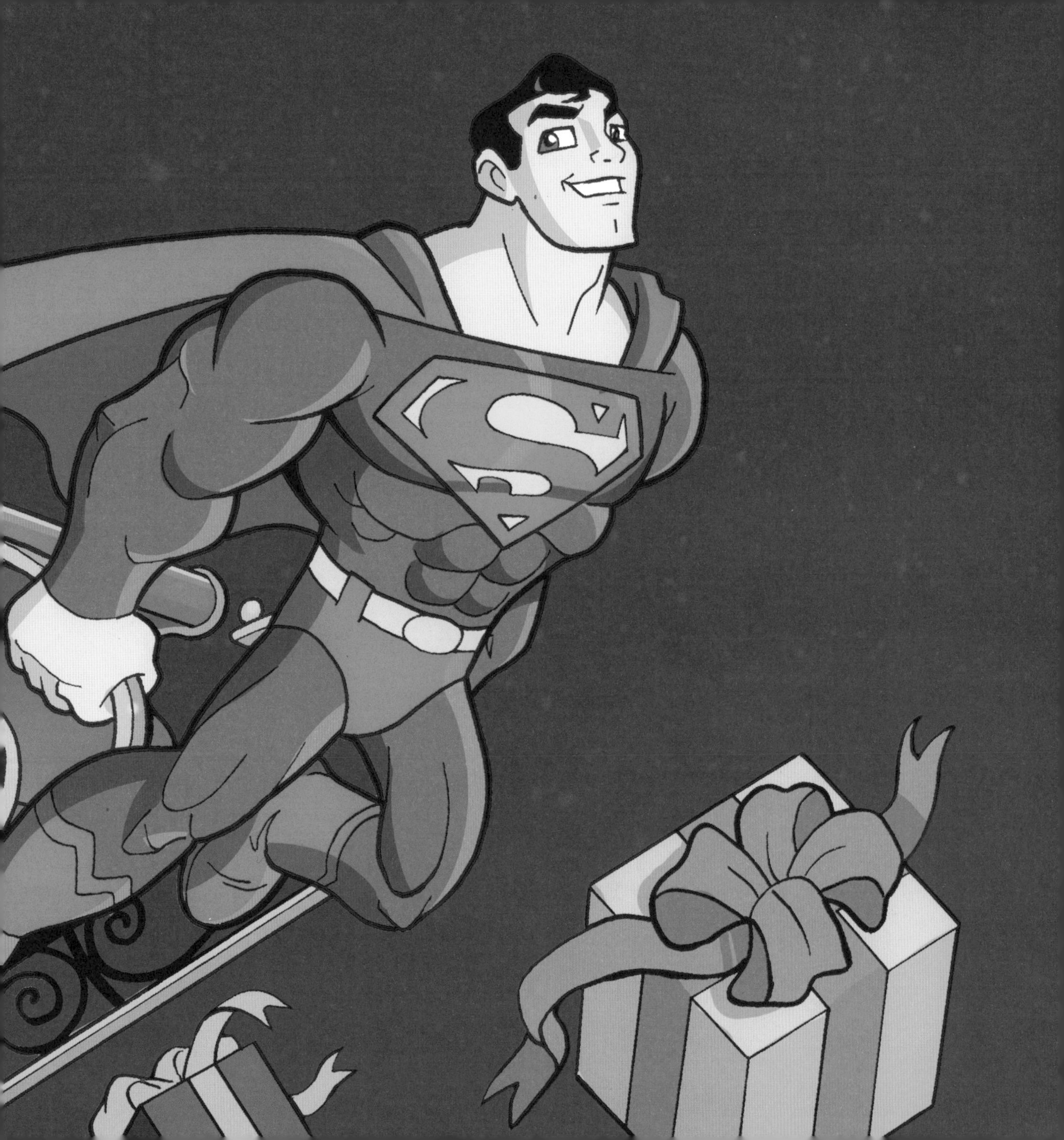

"Thanks, Super Friends," Santa said as happy children everywhere opened their presents. "You saved Christmas!"

"The Super Friends are always ready to lend a hand," Superman replied.

MERRY CHRISTMAS!

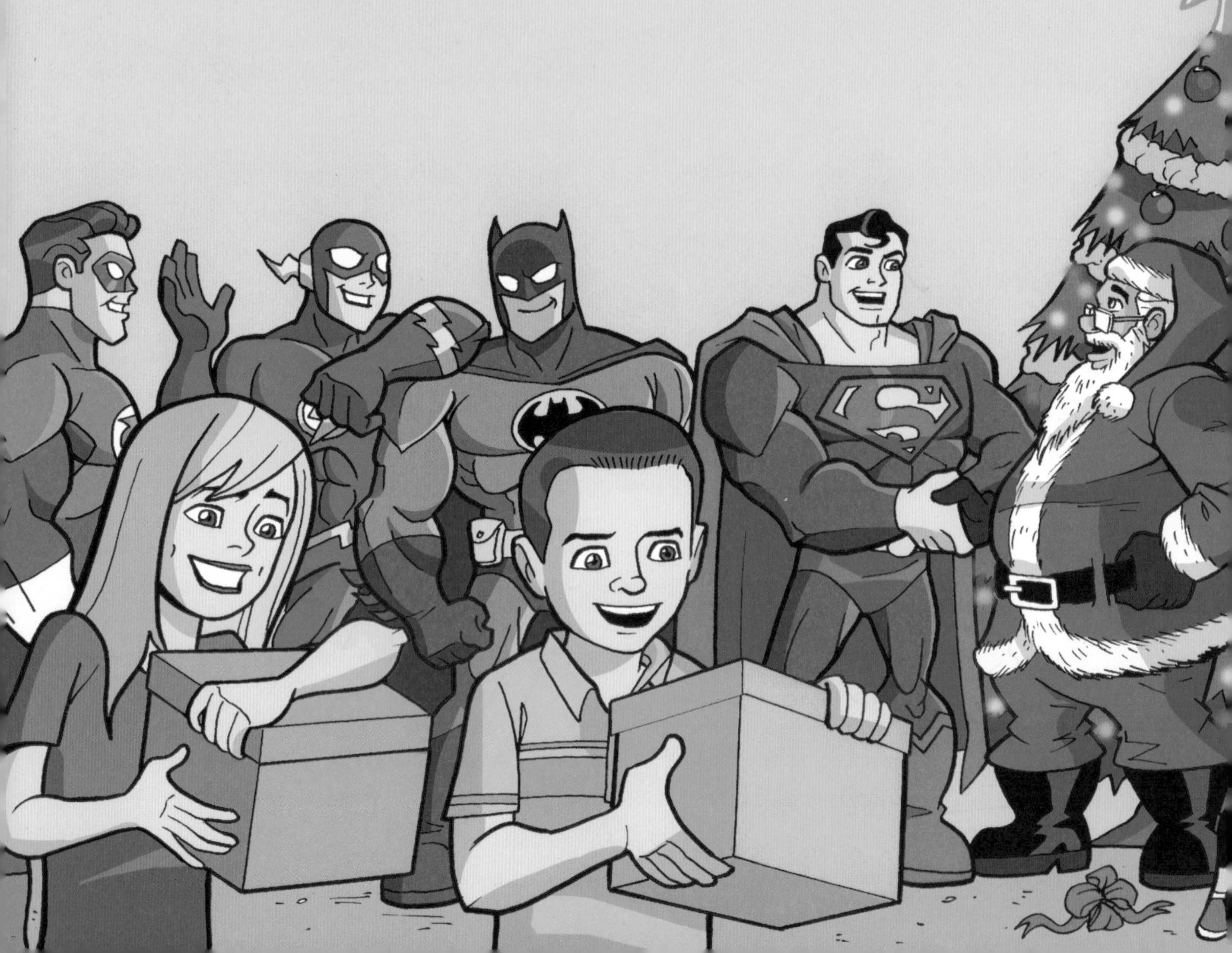

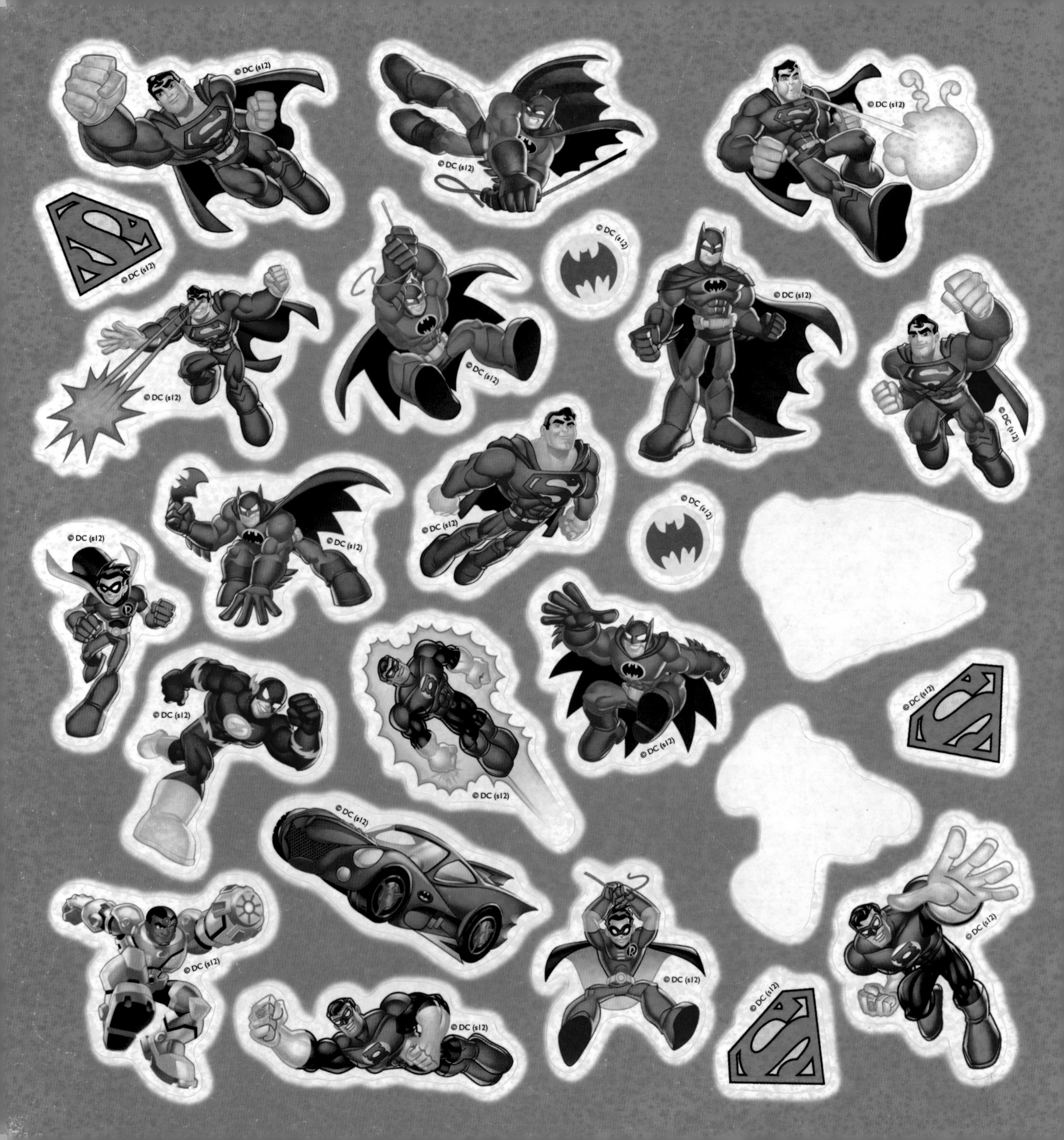
© DC (s12)
© DC (s12)
© DC (s12)
© DC (s12)
© DC (s12)
© DC (s12)
© DC (s12)
© DC (s12)
© DC (s12)
© DC (s12)
© DC (s12)
© DC (s12)
© DC (s12)
© DC (s12)
© DC (s12)
© DC (s12)
© DC (s12)
© DC (s12)
© DC (s12)
© DC (s12)
© DC (s12)
© DC (s12)
© DC (s12)

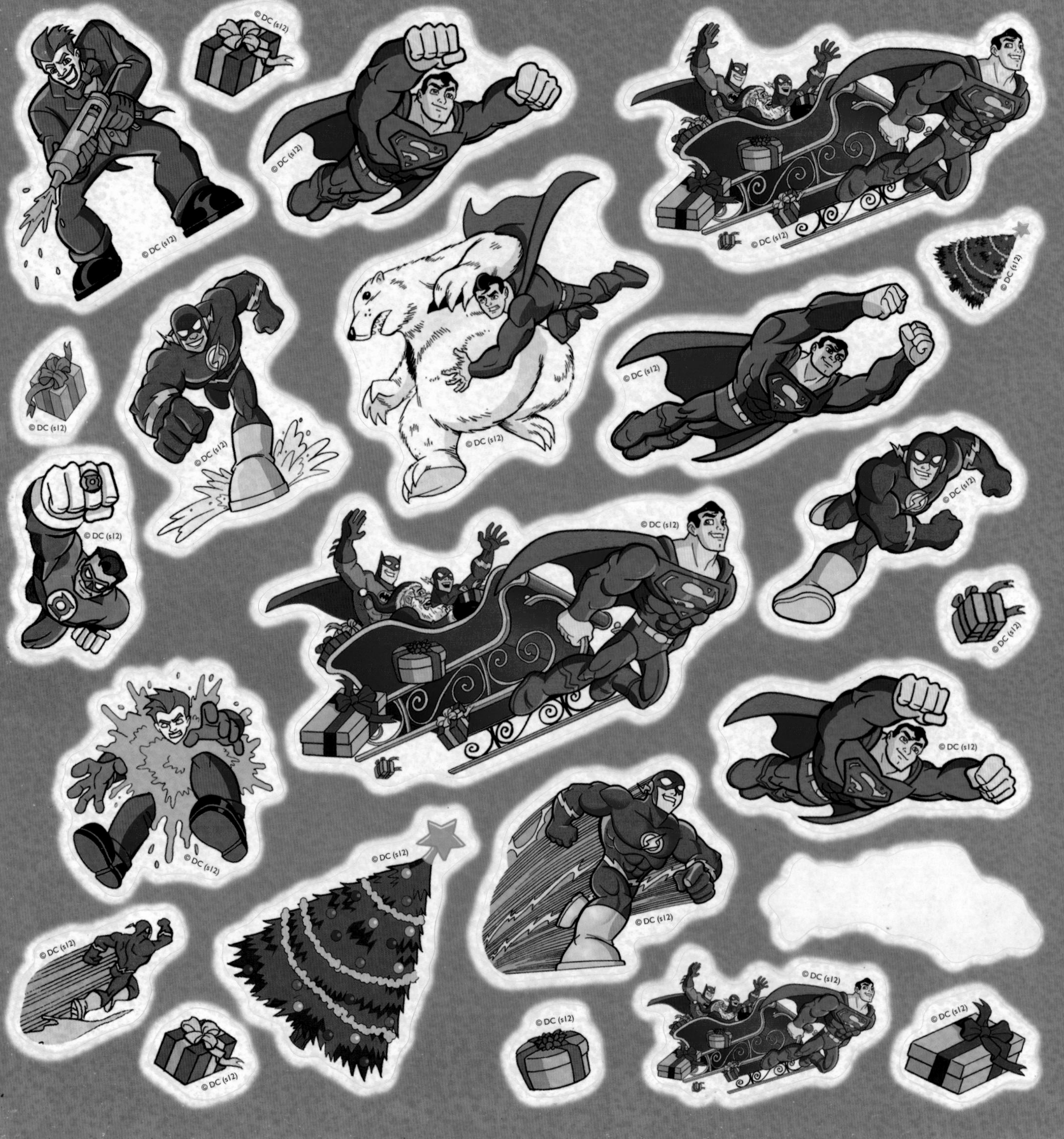
© DC (s12)
© DC (s12)
© DC (s12)
© DC (s12)
© DC (s12)
© DC (s12)
© DC (s12)
© DC (s12)
© DC (s12)
© DC (s12)
© DC (s12)
© DC (s12)
© DC (s12)
© DC (s12)
© DC (s12)
© DC (s12)
© DC (s12)
© DC (s12)
© DC (s12)
© DC (s12)
© DC (s12)
© DC (s12)

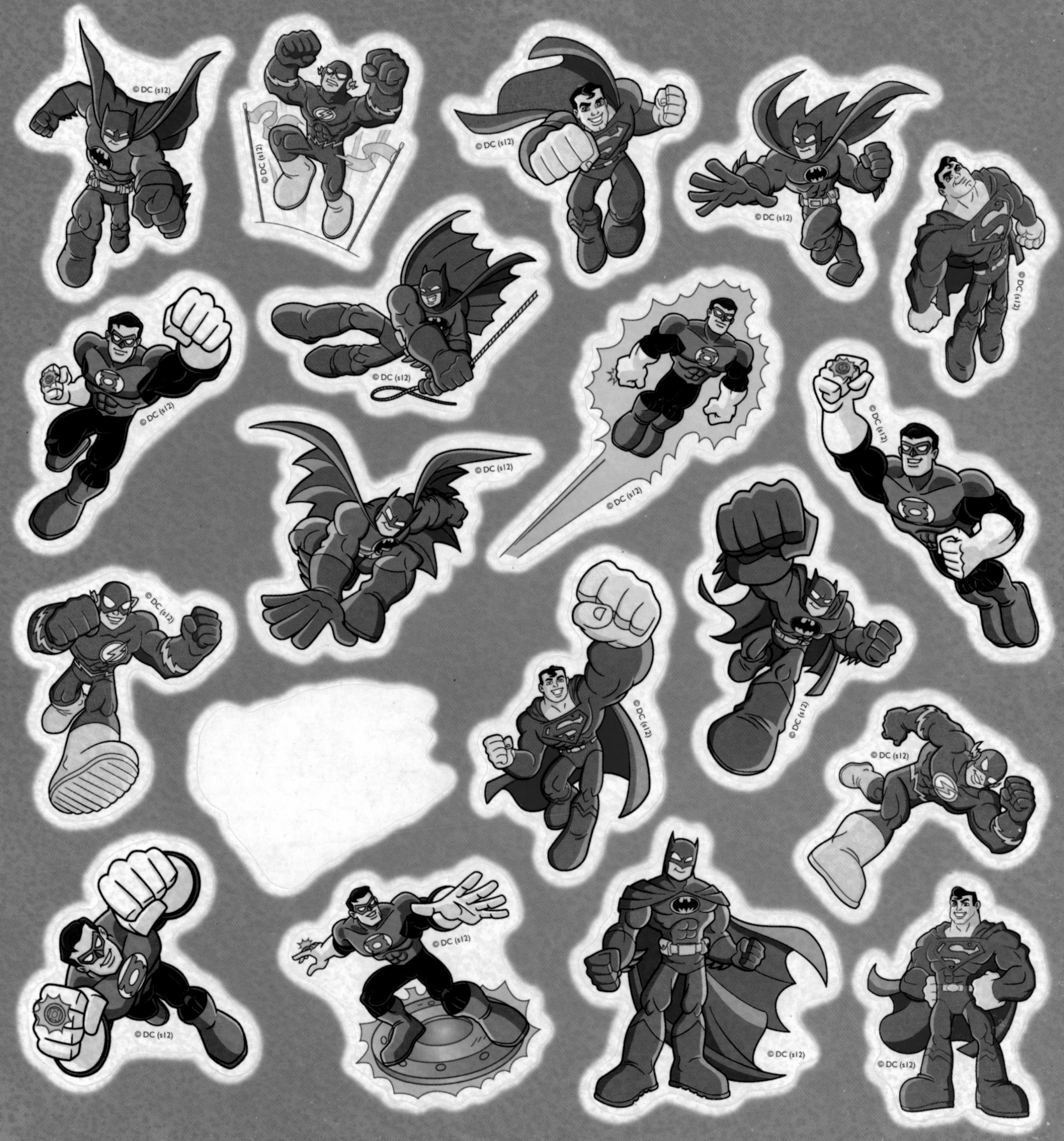
© DC (s12)
© DC (s12)
© DC (s12)
© DC (s12)
© DC (s12)
© DC (s12)
© DC (s12)
© DC (s12)
© DC (s12)
© DC (s12)
© DC (s12)
© DC (s12)
© DC (s12)
© DC (s12)
© DC (s12)
© DC (s12)
© DC (s12)
© DC (s12)

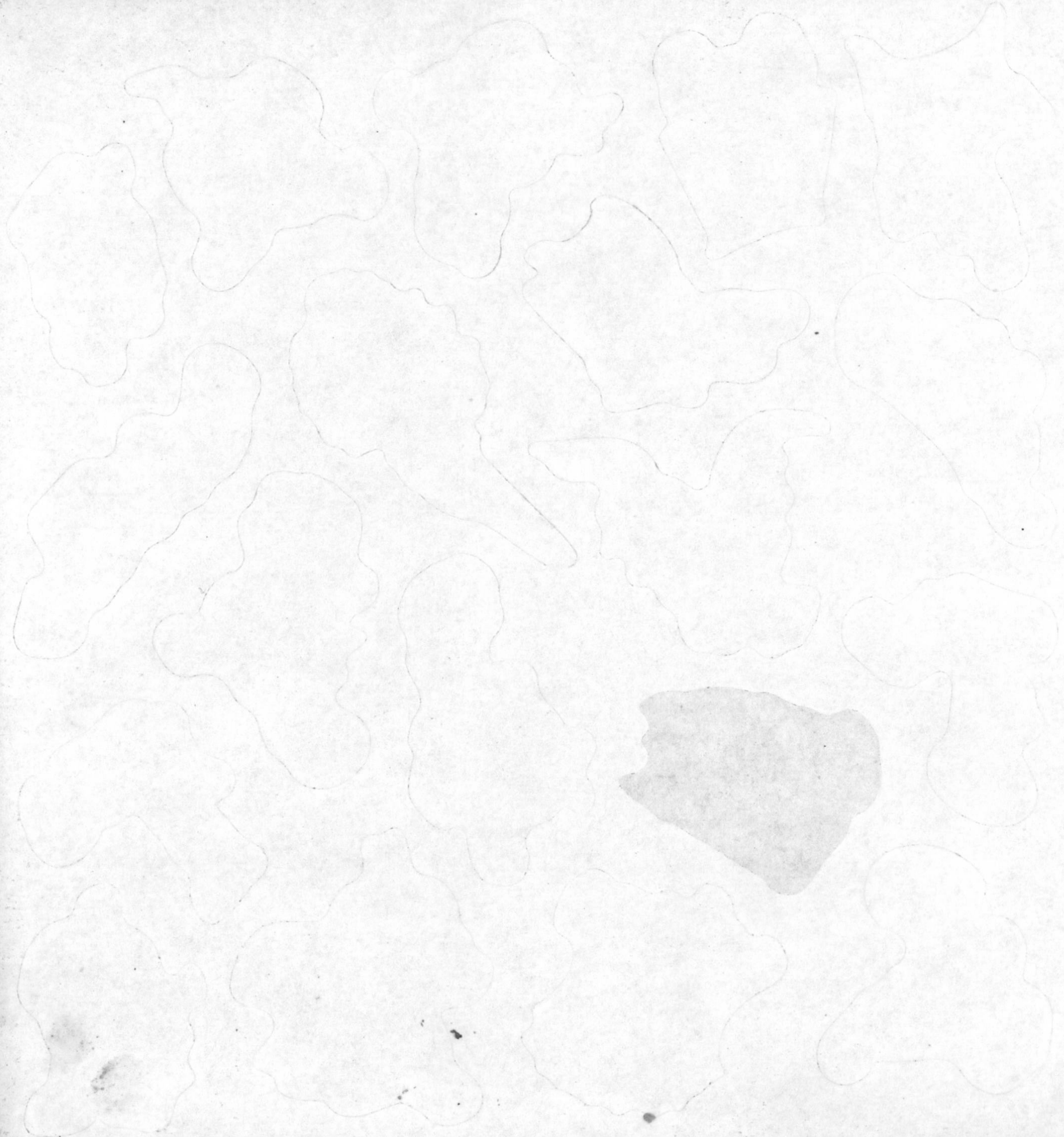

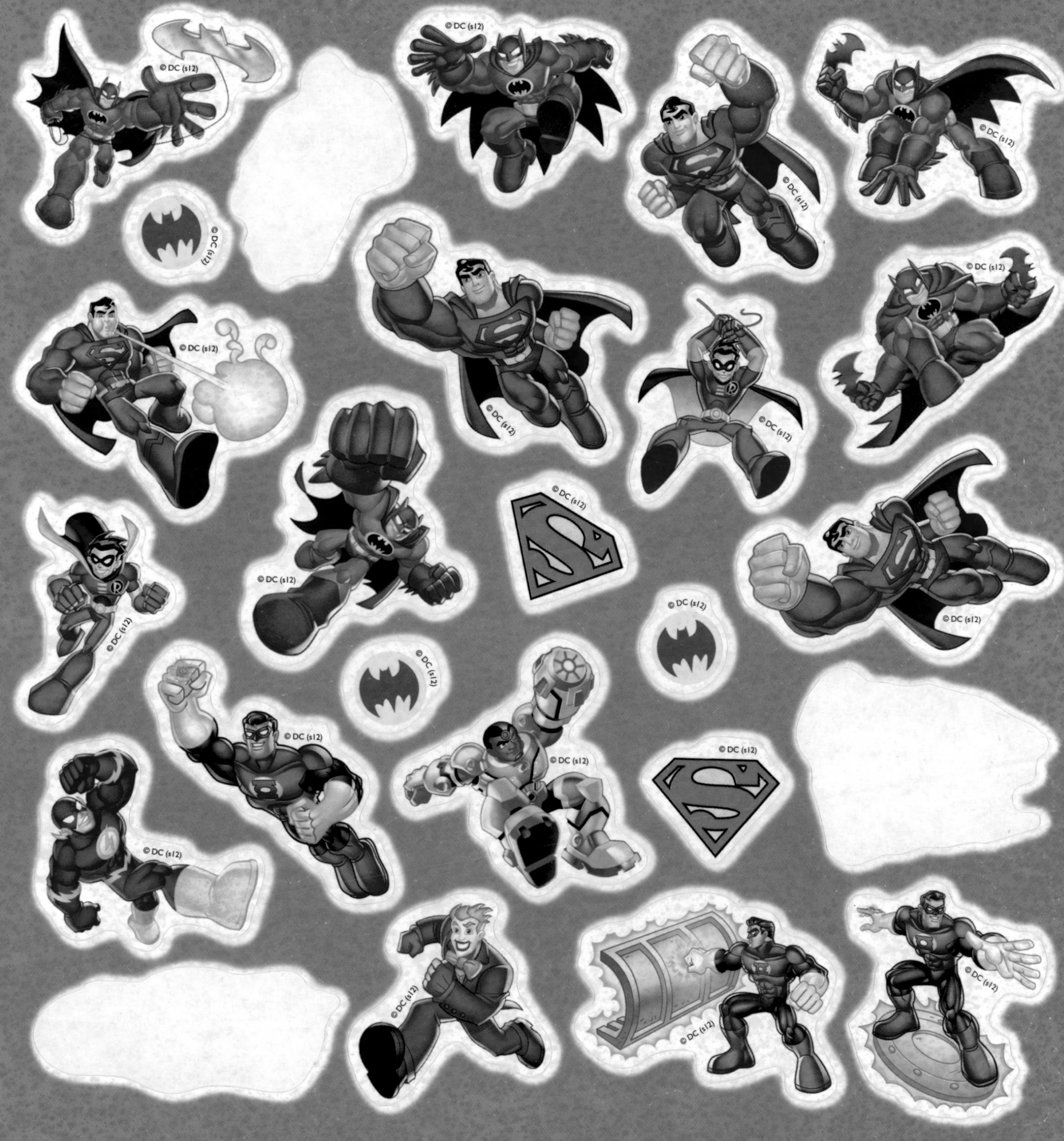
© DC (s12)
© DC (s12)
© DC (s12)
© DC (s12)
© DC (s12)
© DC (s12)
© DC (s12)
© DC (s12)
© DC (s12)
© DC (s12)
© DC (s12)
© DC (s12)
© DC (s12)
© DC (s12)
© DC (s12)
© DC (s12)
© DC (s12)
© DC (s12)
© DC (s12)
© DC (s12)
© DC (s12)
© DC (s12)

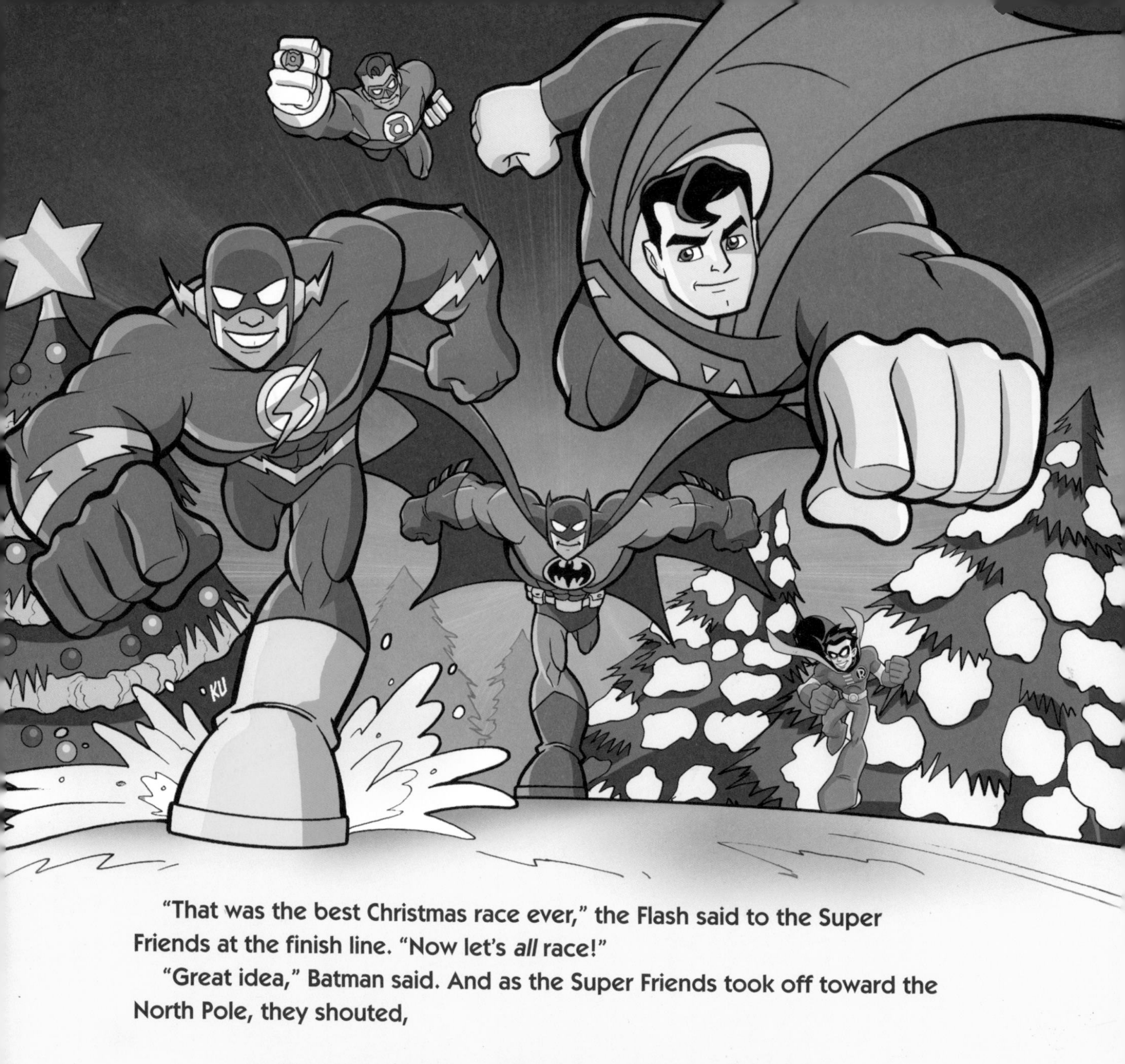
KU

"That was the best Christmas race ever," the Flash said to the Super Friends at the finish line. "Now let's *all* race!"

"Great idea," Batman said. And as the Super Friends took off toward the North Pole, they shouted,

"HAPPY HOLIDAYS!"

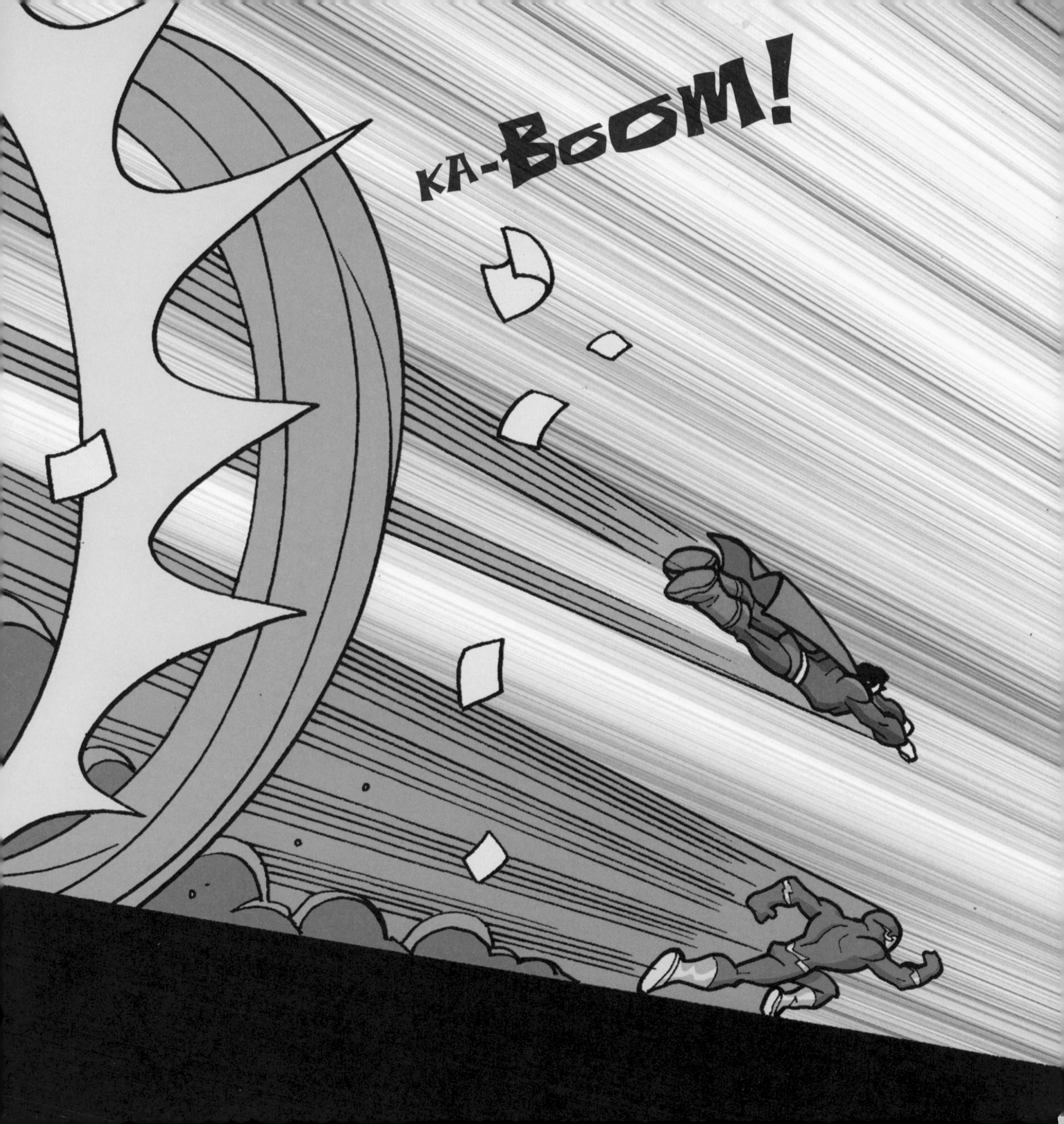
KA-BOOM!

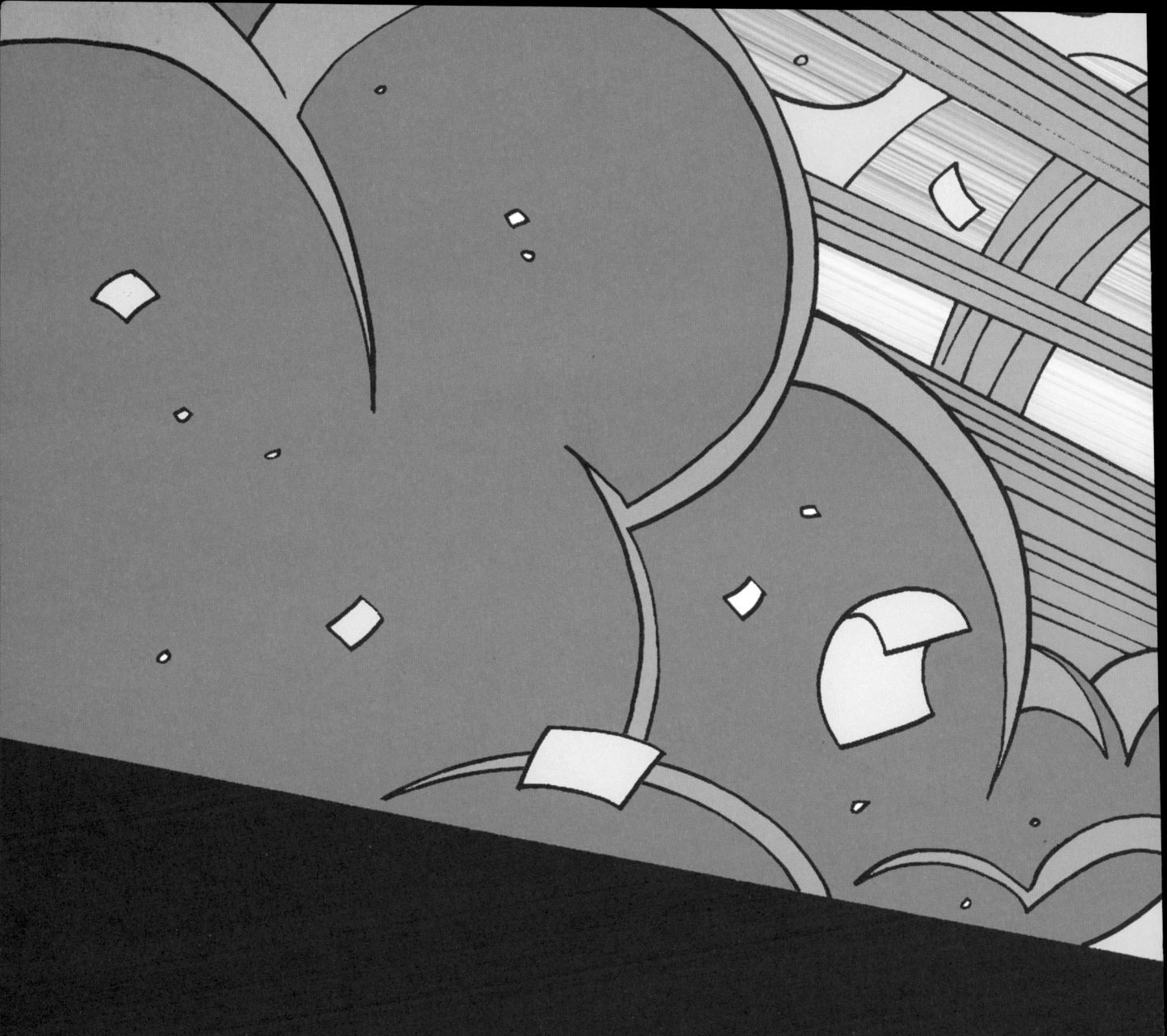

Superman and the Flash raced to the North Pole and then headed back to Metropolis. They were going so fast that they caused a sonic boom! They crossed the finish line together. It was a tie!

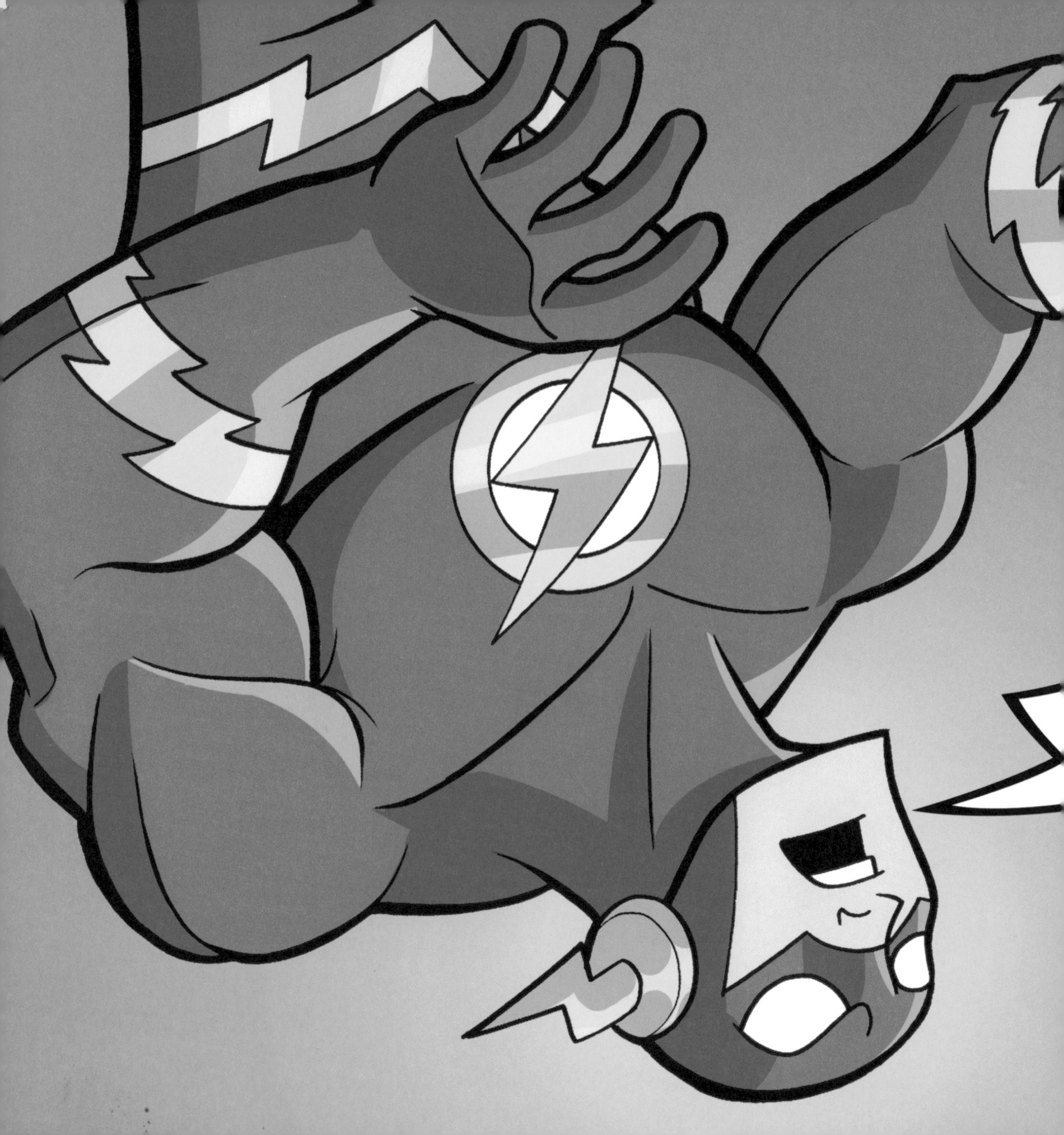

The Flash slowed down and turned around when he found a perfect spot for the polar bear.

"Great work, Superman!" the Flash said as the super-strong hero gently put the polar bear down.

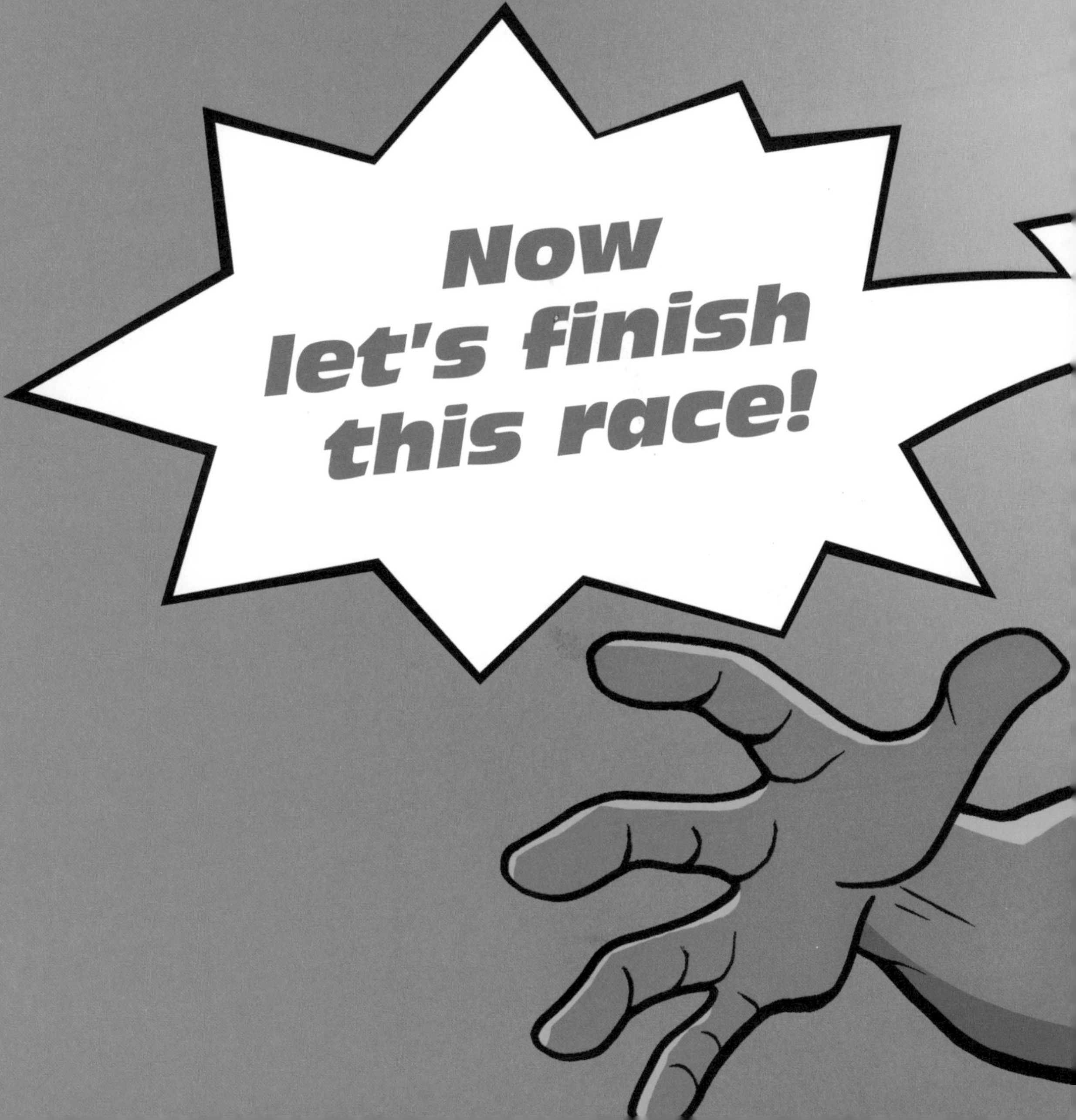
Now let's finish this race!

Soon the heroes discovered the trouble—a polar bear was trapped on a sheet of ice.

"That ice must have floated free while he was sleeping," Superman said, swooping down to pick up the furry polar bear. "Easy, big fella. We're here to help."

"I'll race ahead and find a new home for him on solid ice," the Flash said, pouring on the speed.

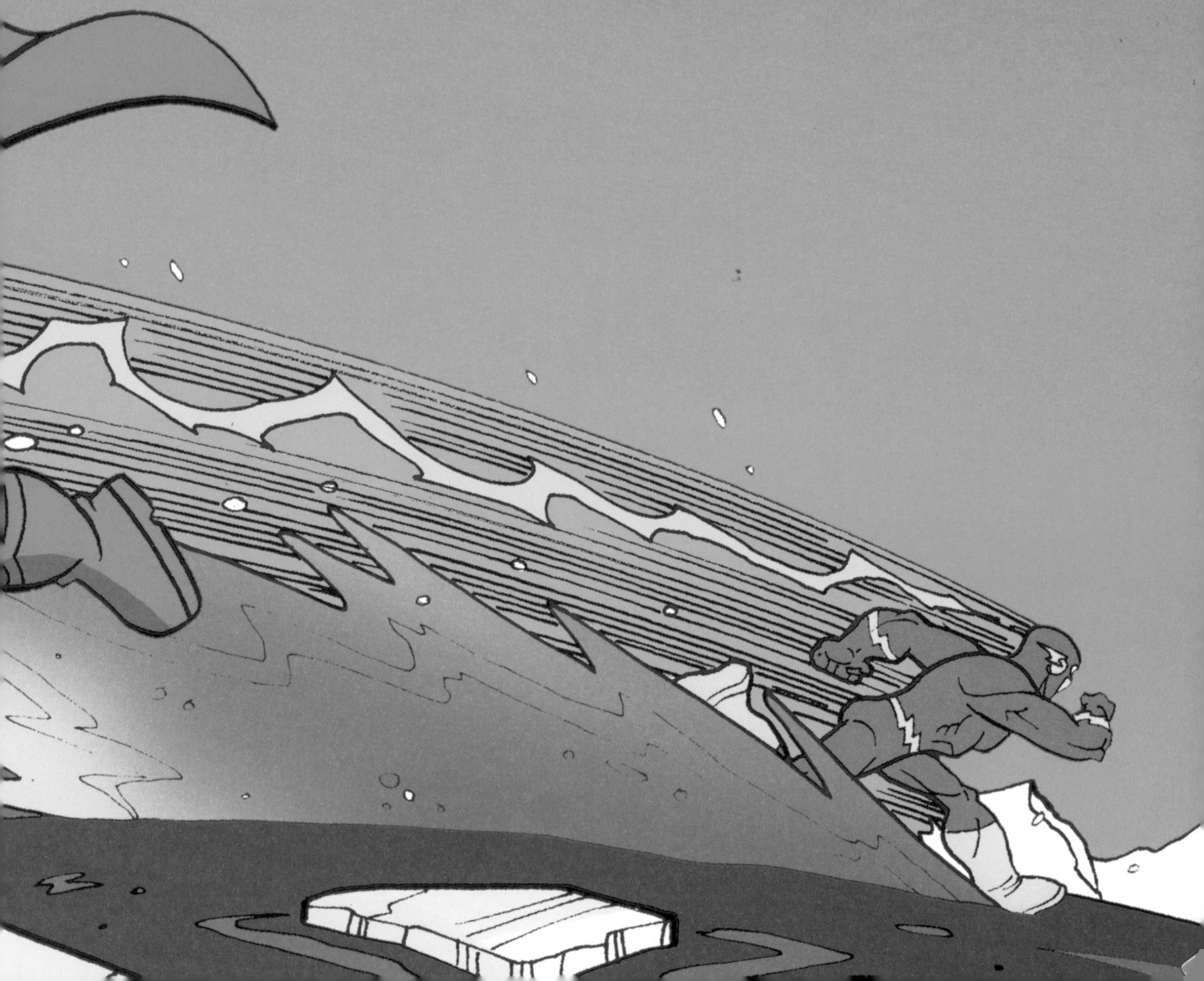

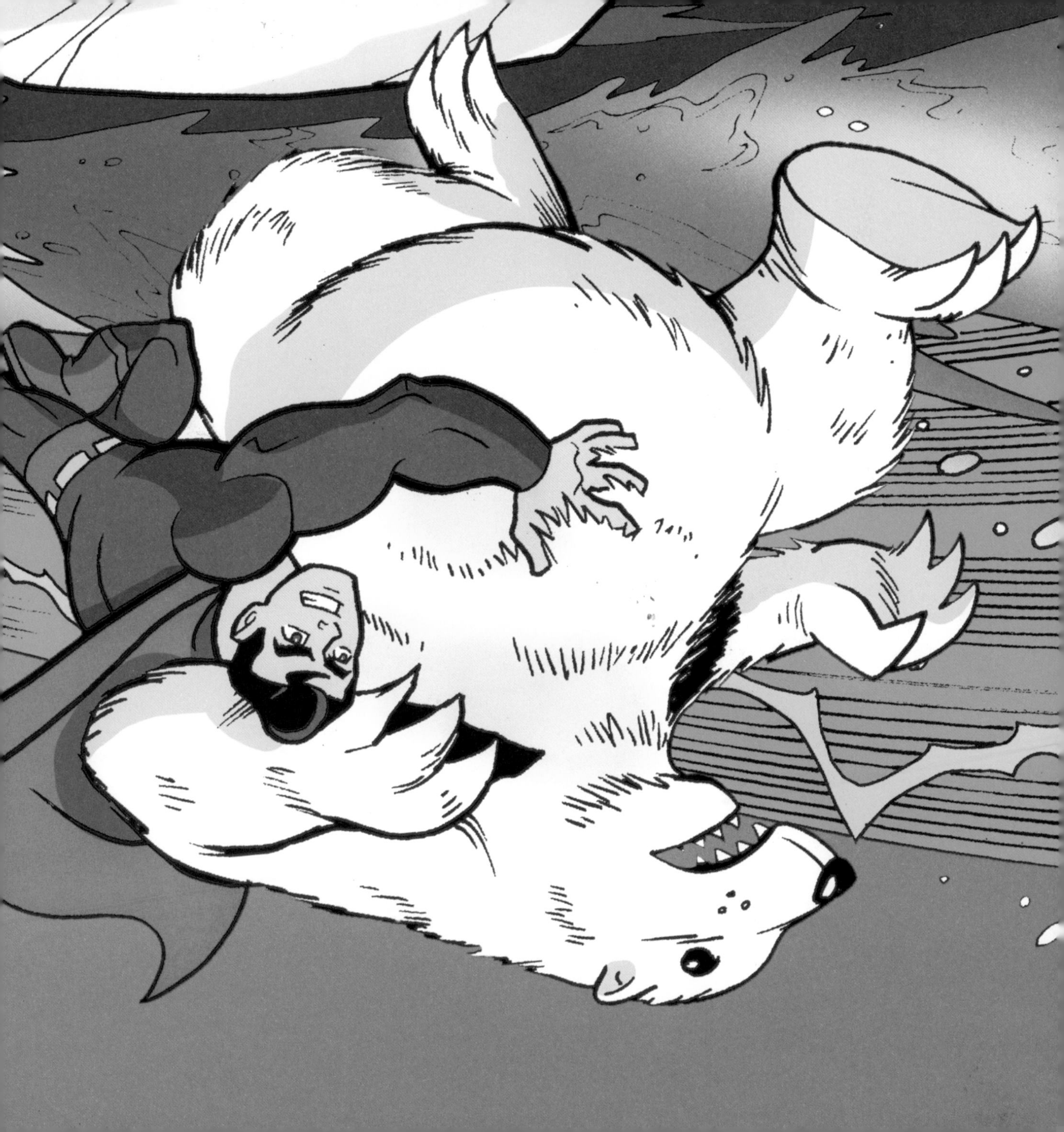

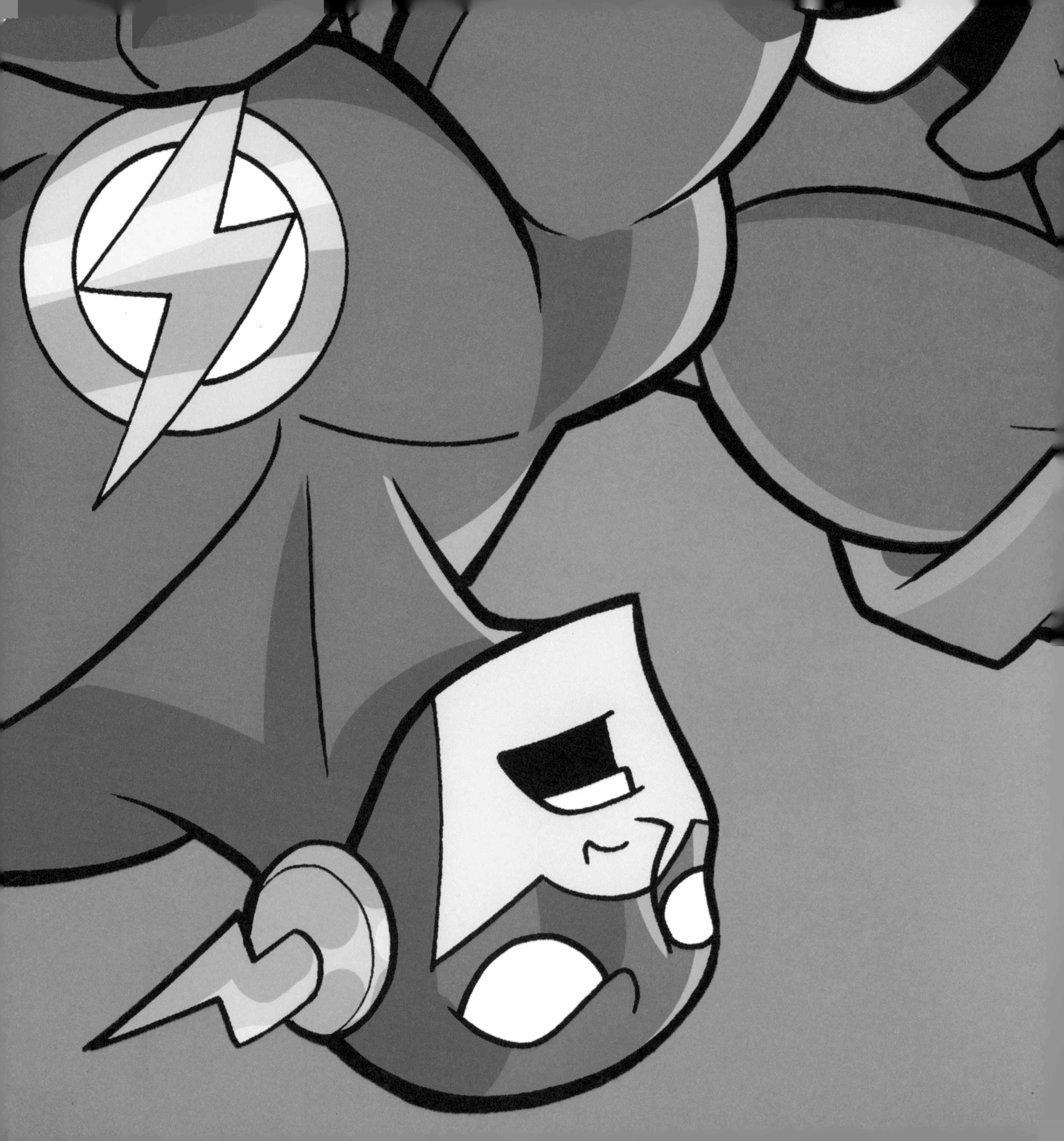

Suddenly, Superman stopped! His super-hearing was picking up something.
"That sounds like someone in distress," Superman said.
"Let's find out who it is and help!" the Flash replied.

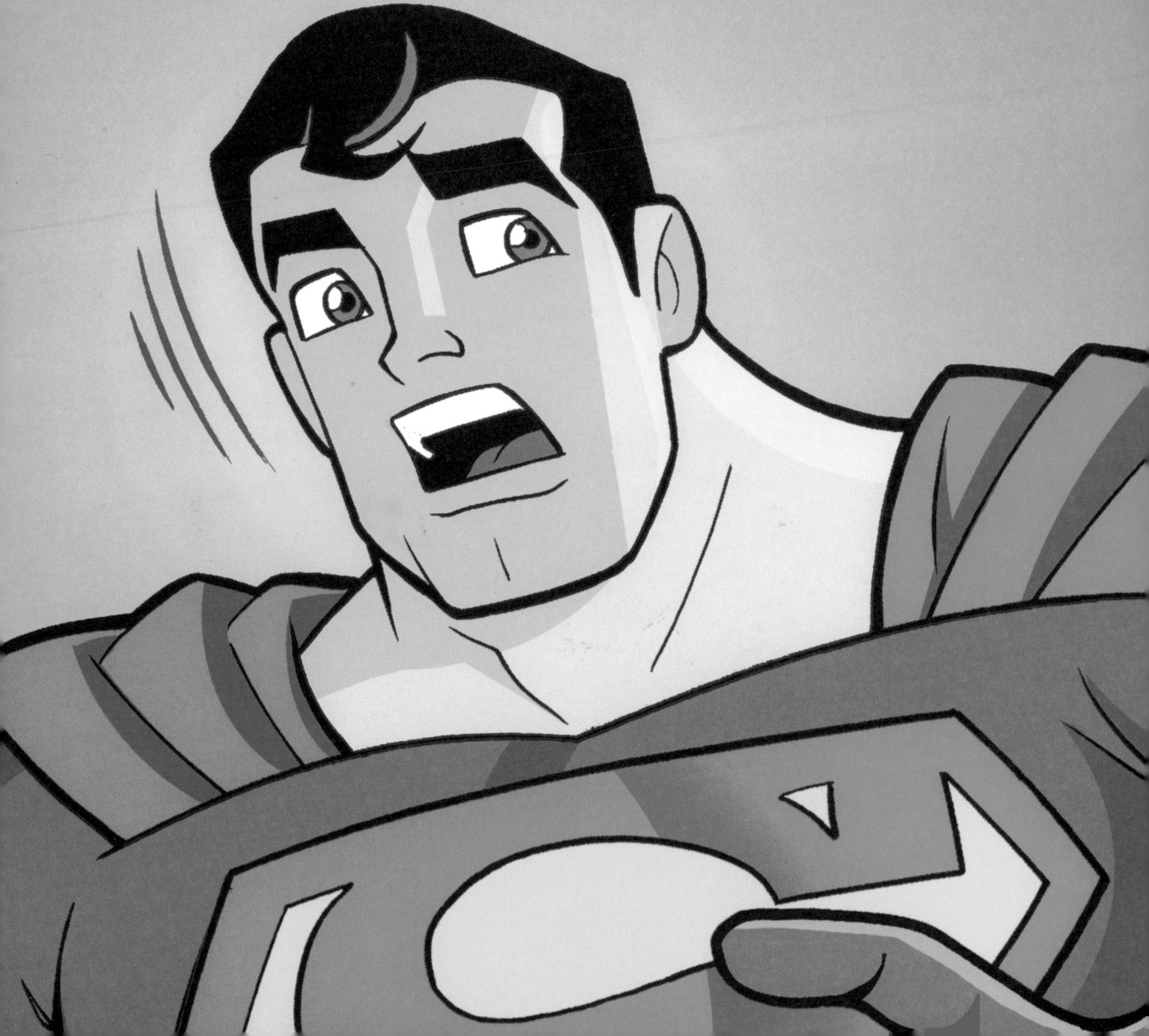

Superman and the Flash raced across the globe at super-speed. Superman could fly over the ocean, but the water didn't stop the Flash. The red-suited hero was so fast, he could run on top of the water! They would be at the North Pole in no time.

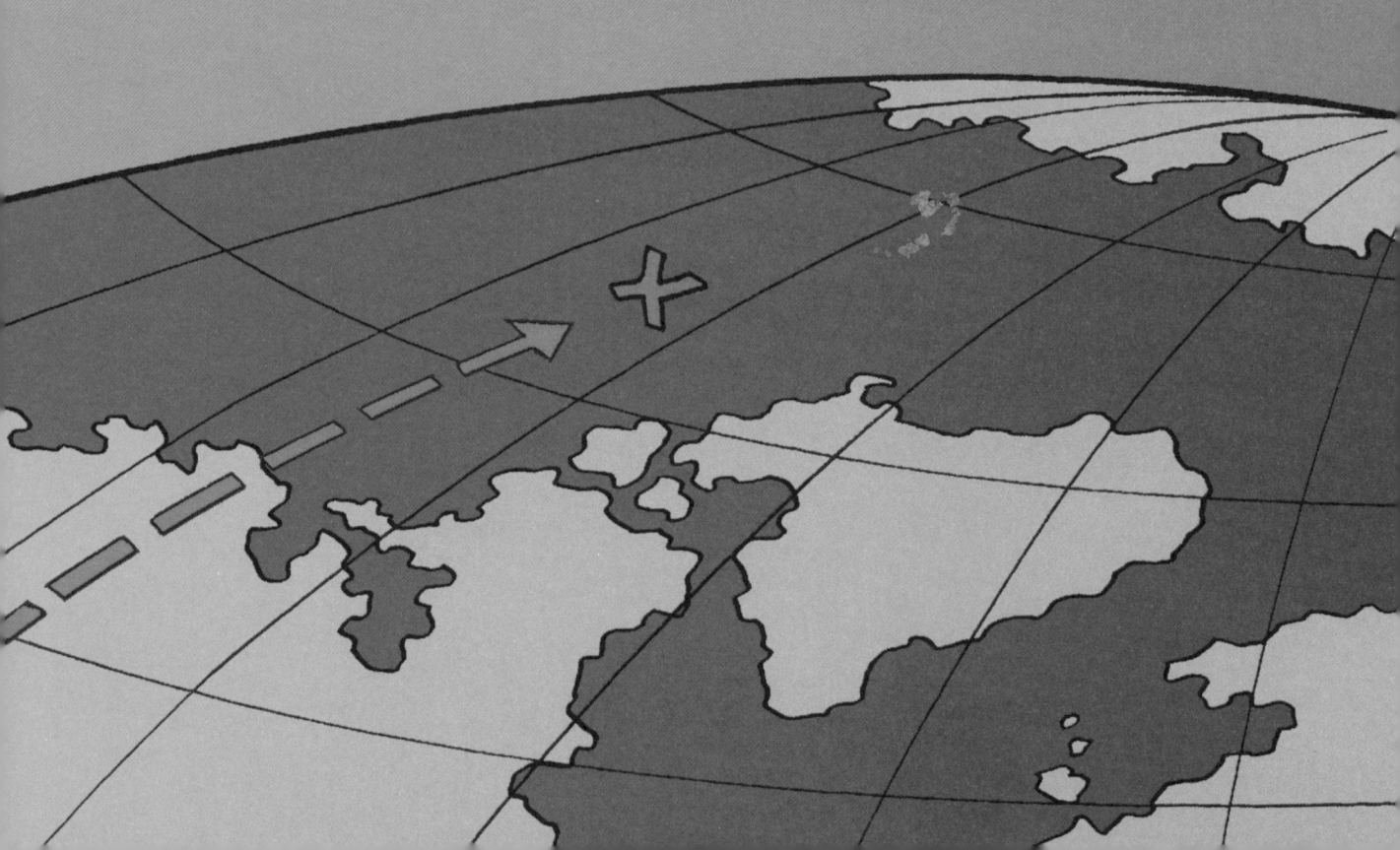

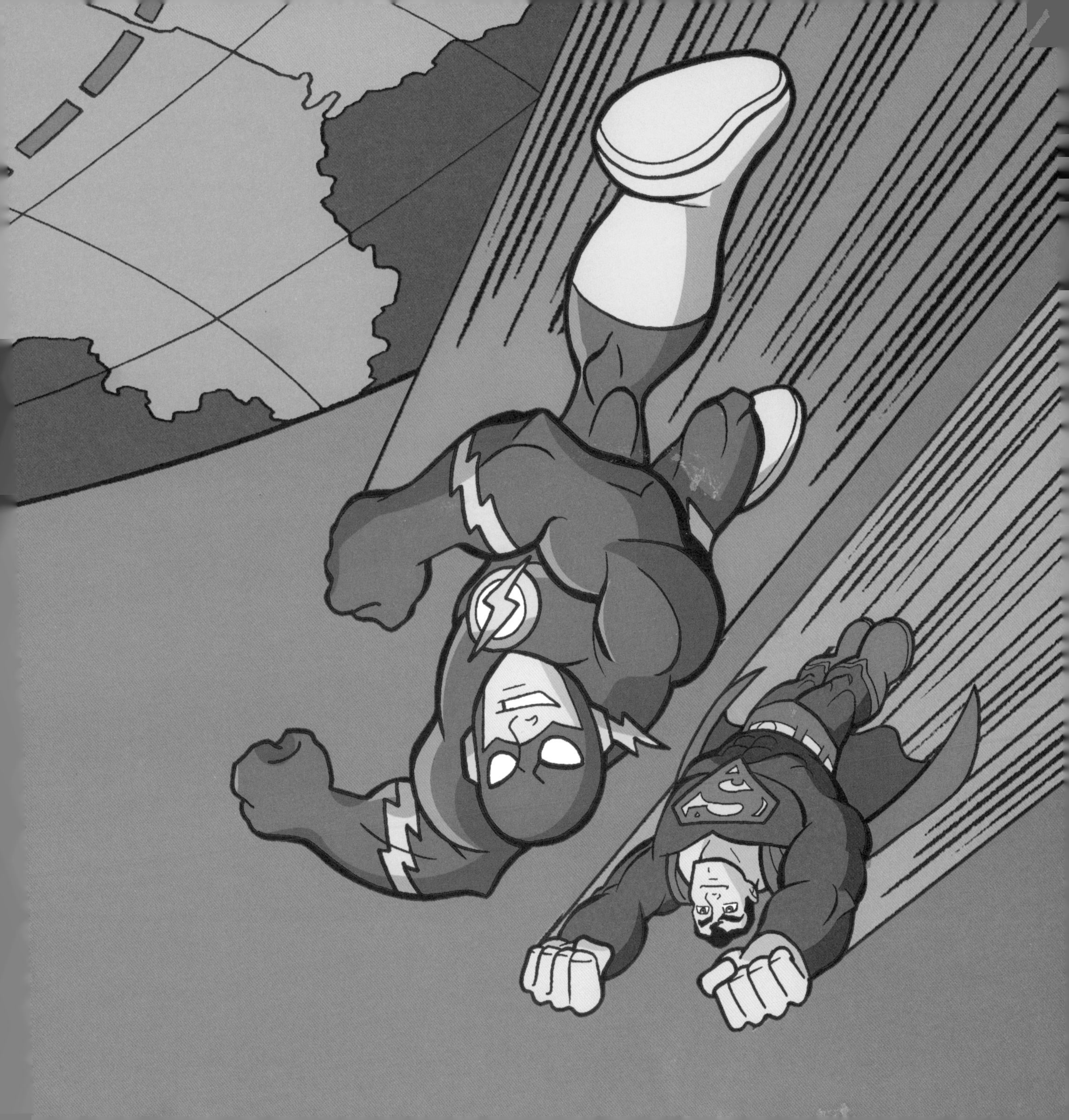

Superman and the Flash took off in a blur of pure speed!

"Let me know if I'm going too fast for you," Superman joked.

"I'm the Fastest Man Alive," the Flash replied with a laugh. "I'll be back and sipping Christmas punch before you even reach the North Pole."

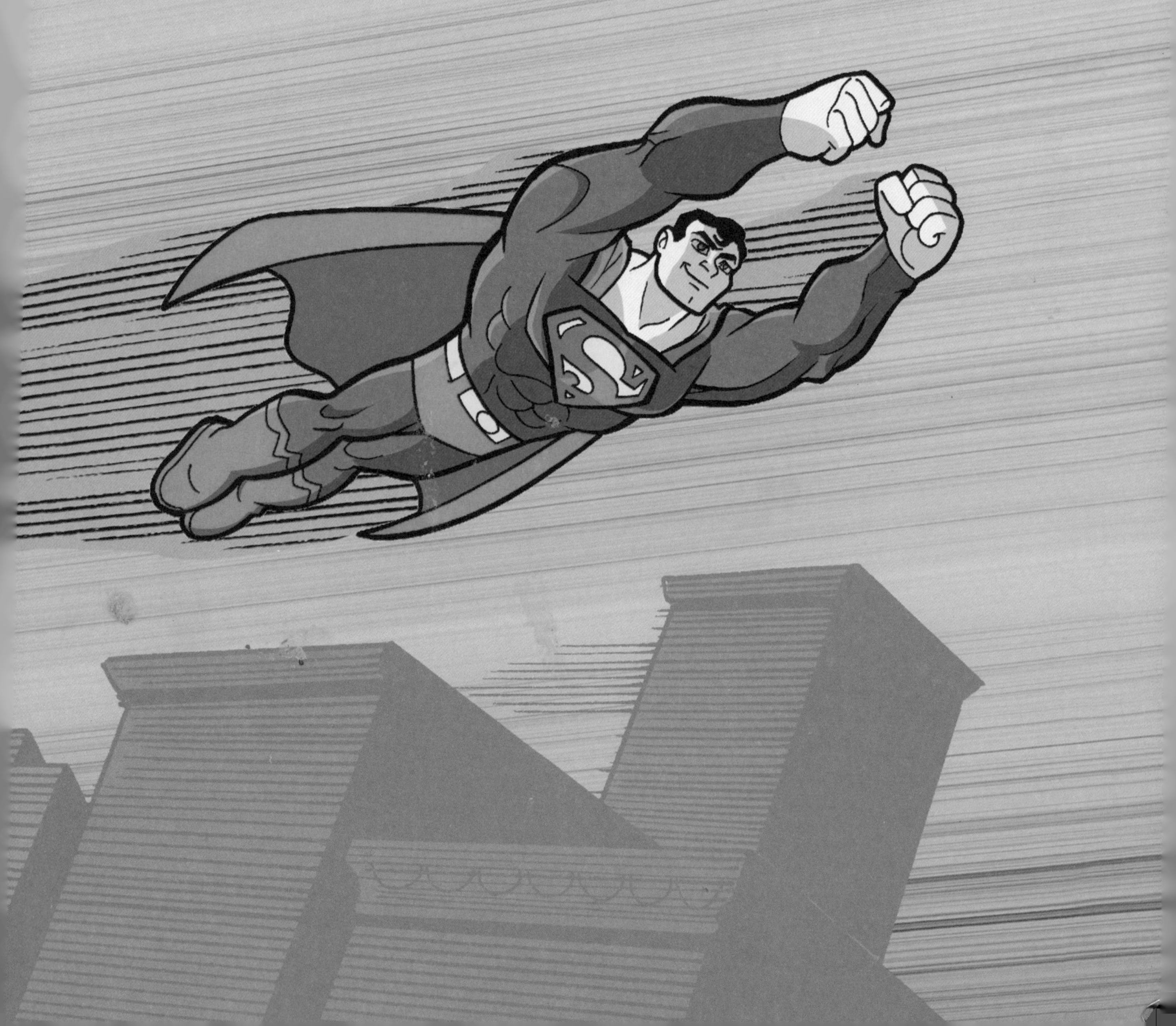

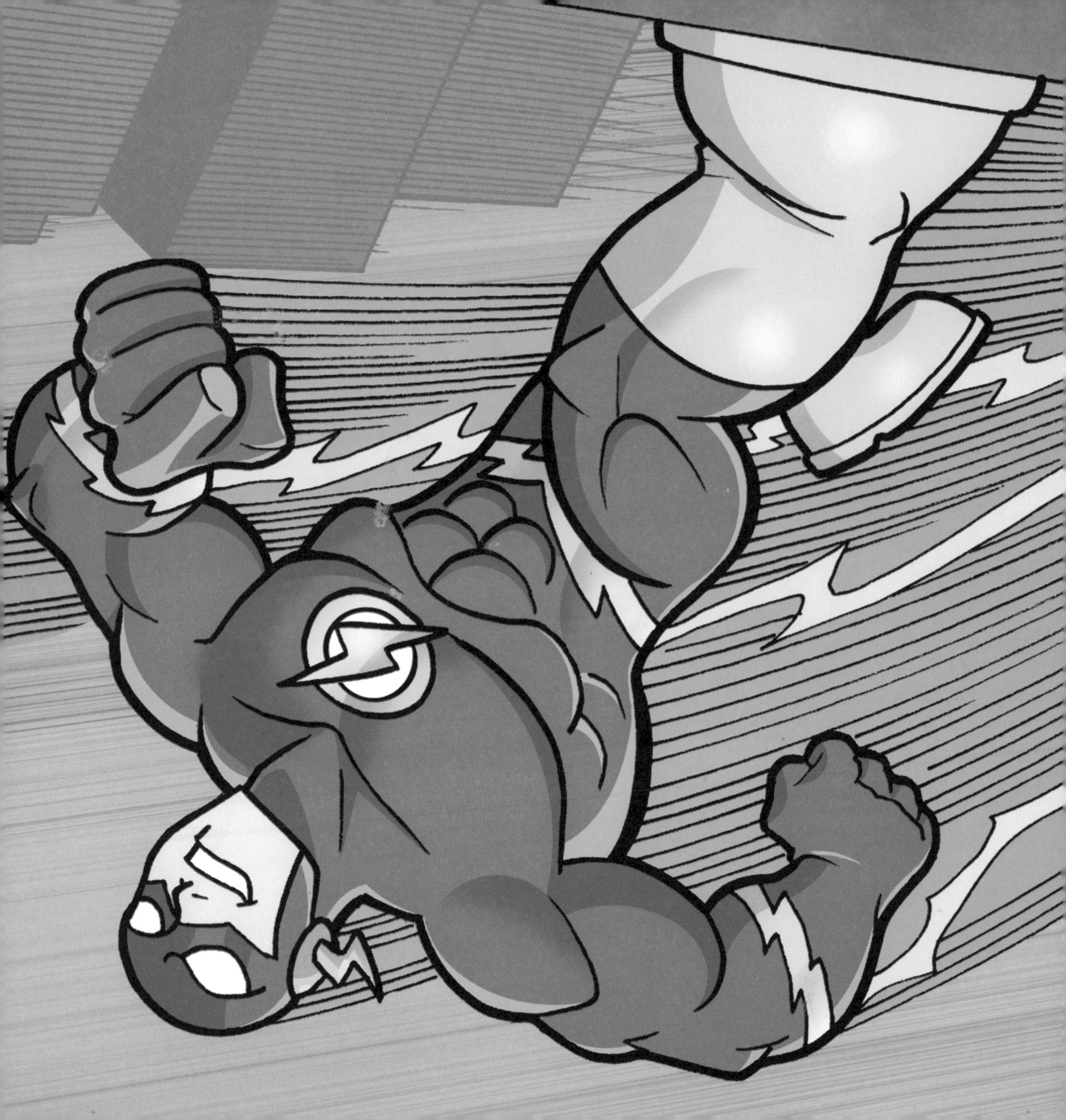

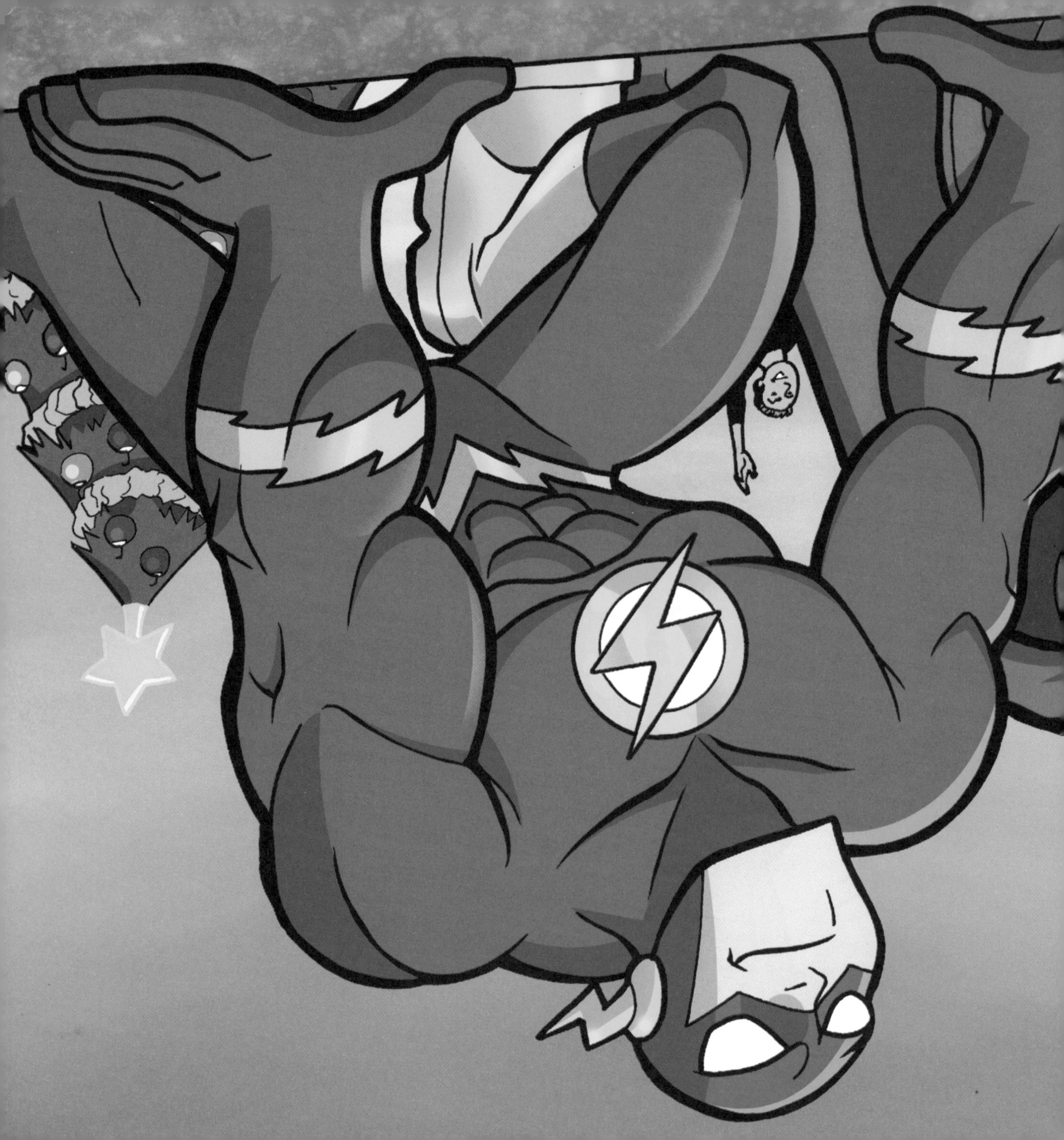

It was Christmastime in Metropolis. Superman and the Flash decided to have a friendly race to raise money for charity.

"This race is to the North Pole and back," Robin said as he raised the starting flag. "Ready! Set! Go!"

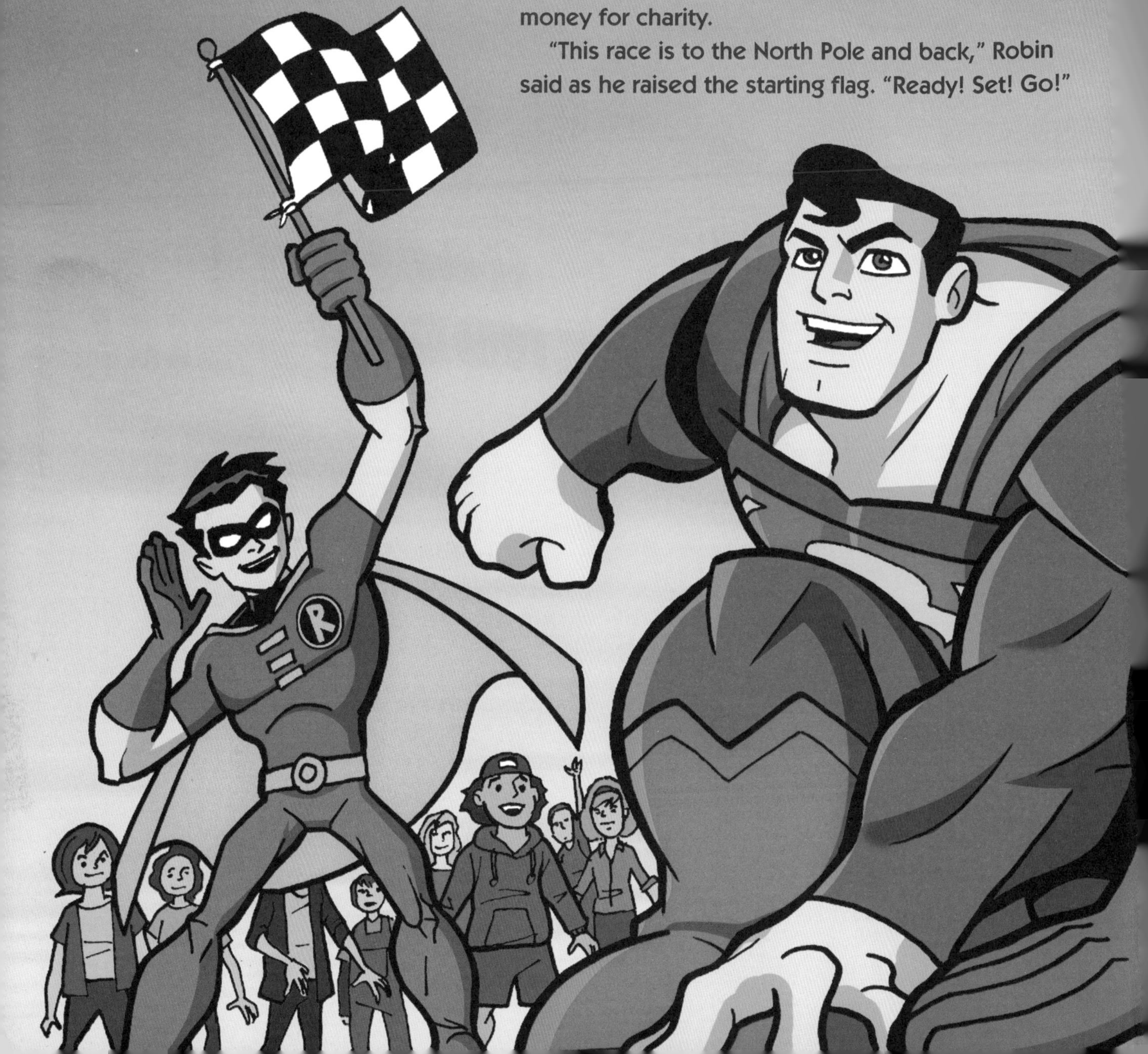

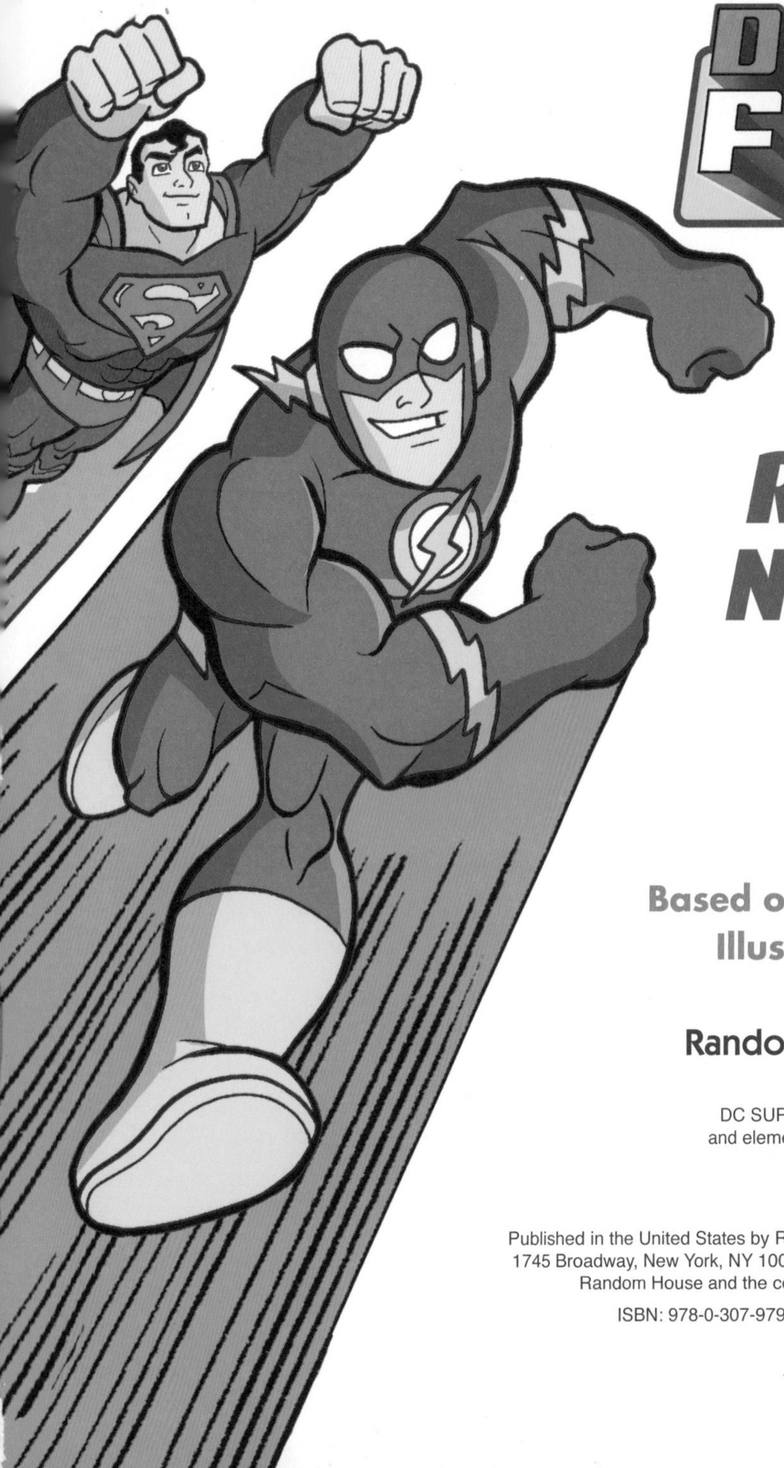

DC SUPER FRIENDS™

RACE TO THE NORTH POLE!

By Billy Wrecks
Based on a story by J. E. Bright
Illustrated by Min S. Ku

Random House New York

RHUS26681

Published in the United States by Random House Children's Books, a division of Random House, Inc., 1745 Broadway, New York, NY 10019, and in Canada by Random House of Canada Limited, Toronto.
Random House and the colophon are registered trademarks of Random House, Inc.

ISBN: 978-0-307-97946-9 randomhouse.com/kids dckids.kidswb.com

MANUFACTURED IN CHINA

10 9 8 7 6 5 4 3 2